Bristol

FRANKENSTEIN'S AUNT

Things up at the old castle have been quiet for years, much to the villagers' relief. But all that changes when a cigar-smoking lady with large feet and a taste for sweet sherry alights from the train at Frankenstein station. Aunt Hanna Frankenstein has returned to the family home.

As the thunder crashes and lightning splits the sky, the villagers tremble at the sight of the frighteningly familiar lights in the castle laboratory. Aunt Hanna, her odd assistant Igor and male secretary Frans are trying to revive Henry's monster – to help Aunt Hanna with the gardening and the housework. But the local people are in for an even more hair-raising time when the strange Mr Talbot, and his old friend Count Dracula arrive on the scene...

Frankenstein's Aunt

Allan Rune Pettersson

Translated by Joan Tate

HEINEMANN
NEW WINDMILLS

Heinemann Educational Books Ltd
Halley Court, Jordan Hill, Oxford OX2 8EJ
OXFORD   LONDON   EDINBURGH
MADRID   ATHENS   BOLOGNA   PARIS
MELBOURNE   SYDNEY   AUCKLAND
IBADAN   NAIROBI   HARARE   GABORONE
SINGAPORE   TOKYO   PORTSMOUTH NH (USA)

ISBN 0 435 12260 6

91 92 93 94 15 14 13 12 11 10 9 8

Printed in England by Clays Ltd, St Ives plc

Contents

Next Stop Frankenstein

The train whistle shrilled through the night like a scream of terror.

The old lady in the smoking compartment leant forward to look out of the window. She still couldn't see anything, for the window was steamed up and streaked with rain, the night outside as black as soot. Smoke from the engine now and again swirled down round the carriage, making her feel she was being driven through the clouds. Lightning flashed across the sky, for a moment revealing bare wet mountain peaks and thick black pine-forests. Then it was dark again, not a single light from a human dwelling to be seen. The train rattled on through the night, the claps of the thunder drowned by the thumpety-thump of the wheels on the rails.

The old lady leant back and lit a cigar. She was beginning to get thoroughly fed up with this journey. If only her secretary had come with her, as had been decided from the start, but he was in bed at home with yet another cold. 'He ought to see a specialist about all those colds,' she thought irritably. And then the railway company had the nerve to call this *first* class, which she thought was nothing but a mockery to an old person. The seats were dreadfully saggy and the lighting quite beyond the pale, one single little bulb in a bell-shaped pink shade spreading a dim trembling light over the compartment. It was almost impossible even to think of reading. Several times she had tried to make some kind of sense out of the notes her nephew had left behind, but it was impossible in this light. The boy was certainly good at making a mess of things, anyhow, that much she had managed to fathom.

Of course, Henry had always been pretty hopeless as a child, but that as an adult he should have had the idea of putting together a monster from pieces of dead people! What an idea! Distasteful, too. But scientists and soldiers were all the same, and she had both kinds in her family. They never really grew up. To scientists and soldiers, life was just one long holiday among test-tubes and tin soldiers. Or that was what she thought.

She picked up the yellowing sheaf of papers from her lap and tried again. She found a place that defied even the dim light and read with rising excitement:

One lovely stormy night with the rain drumming against the window-panes, my work was completed. He was lying there, the first human being ever created by human hand. I shiver as I write, when I consider the extent of my deed. In charnel-houses and churchyards, by the light of flickering candles in musty tombs, I had gathered the material for this creation in the most ungodly way. I had done my best to give him friendly and pleasant features. I had stitched and patched day and night, but now there he was, still bandaged from head to foot, not unlike a mummy, and then I was filled with horror at the thought that I might have failed. Trembling with anxiety, I got my instruments ready to bring a spark of life to my creation . . .

At that moment, the train again whistled shrilly and the old lady reckoned it was good to know the Monster had been lying harmless for a decade under tons of stone

8

up there in the ruined laboratory. She drew deeply on her cigar and went on reading:

How can I describe my feelings as the bandages fell away and he finally opened his eyes? Beautiful? Had I thought I'd made him beautiful! His yellow skin scarcely stretched over his bones and sinews, as if I had tried to sew a far too large body into a patchwork of too small clothes. And that head I'd worked so hard on! I had tried to give him a high intellectual forehead, and the forehead was high enough all right, but far too high, and his hair was hanging down in black straggles from his much too flat skull. But he was breathing! He was alive! And he was looking at me with his watery eyes, the puckered skin on his face twitching, the thin black lips opening . . .

'Next stop Frankenstein!'

The guard had thrust his drooping yellow moustache in through the compartment door, coughing at the cigar smoke billowing out to meet him and peering suspiciously from under the peak of his cap. Oh, this eternal malevolence that affected the whole family! 'The scoundrel,' thought the old lady, about her nephew, who was to blame for everything.

'Well, about time, too,' she said, majestically rising to her full height, cigar ash tumbling from her black travelling costume as she crushed the cigar butt beneath the heel of her boot. The guard noticed that his own shoes were at least five sizes smaller and that he came just about up to her shoulder as they stood there.

'Can I get a porter at the station, do you think, my man?'

'Shouldn't think so, Missis. Not at this hour of night.'

The old lady thought she caught a glimpse of a malicious smile beneath the old man's yellow moustache.

'Then I'll just have to manage,' she said, letting her

9

suitcase fall with a thump at his feet. 'Unless the Monster comes to meet me . . .' she added with a wry little smile.

The compartment door slammed shut and the guard vanished.

The whistle shrilled again and the train slowed down. The old lady pressed her nose against the window, but the darkness was just as close. She started hauling her luggage out into the corridor.

The train stopped with a jerk, the steam hissing out. One single passenger alighted from the first class carriage, a smoking compartment, and climbed down the steps into the pouring rain. Lightning lit up the station, a modest grey wooden building with rain-water gushing out of the drainpipes. Lightning also lit up the notice above the waiting-room, showing the name that a few decades ago had spread terror and sudden death far and wide.

𝔉𝔯𝔞𝔫𝔨𝔢𝔫𝔰𝔱𝔢𝔦𝔫

The name made a rather feeble impression now, the old lady thought, but perhaps that was just because the notice could have done with a lick of paint.

As soon as the guard had seen her name on the ticket, he had started behaving differently towards her, and she regretted letting the travel agency write out her itinerary. She should have bought one of those ordinary little anonymous bits of cardboard instead, of course. They didn't tell other people who she was. The guard had not been exactly unfriendly, but he had been very much on his guard, like a lion-tamer who dared not turn his back on the lion.

Before her journey, she had often wondered whether she would be met with the same great crowd of umbrellas or the same excited sea of torchlight that had often greeted her nephew. But when she stepped off the train, she saw that she needn't have worried. Not a single umbrella, nor a single torch, nor a single voice yelling at her to go back home. The only things to meet her were a flash of lightning, a soaking wet platform, a clap of thunder, and rain–filled darkness.

The train had already moved off again, the engine coughing steam and spitting sparks, the carriages jerking. The guard was just mounting the steps to his door, and he gave the old lady one long last look before he slid past her into the rain.

She felt like sticking her tongue out at him, but controlled herself at the last moment. The family reputation was bad enough already because of that wretched Henry. She had come here to try to retrieve for the old family name some of its previous fame, and she had no intention of concealing the connection.

She picked up her cases and walked over to the ticket-office, where she had seen a faint light. So the village wasn't quite dead.

A short distance away, hidden in the darkest spot, someone was watching her ...

Igor

The old lady rapped on the glass of the ticket-office and a shadow appeared on the blind behind. The blind rushed up, the hatch opened and the station-master looked out. He was a thin man with a shiny bald head, a green shade on his forehead.

'Yes?' he said in a thin voice, scratching under one arm.

The old lady noticed there was a half-empty bottle of sherry on the counter.

'I hope that's dry,' she said, pointing a long bony finger through the opening. 'Or at least medium-dry.'

The station-master started and hurriedly hid the bottle, as if he had been caught drinking on duty.

'I prefer sweet sherry,' he said, a trifle self-consciously. Then his voice sharpened. 'Is there anything I can do for you?' He fiddled irritably with his green shade and scratched under the other arm.

'If there's a telephone in the ticket-office, I should be grateful if you would telephone for a cab,' said the old lady.

'A cab?' said the station-master grumpily. He did not consider it his business to telephone for cabs at half-past eleven at night.

But he stretched out his hand for the telephone and sulkily wound the handle for the operator.

'What was the name?'

'Hanna Frankenstein,' the old lady said slowly, articulating very clearly.

The man's eyes widened under the green shade.

The next moment, the ticket-hatch had slammed down and the blind was pulled down. On the shadow on the blind, Hanna Frankenstein saw the station-master taking a great gulp of sherry straight out of the bottle.

She was just about to knock on the glass again, determined not to stand for any more of this nonsense, when someone touched her arm.

She turned round.

A tiny little old hunchback was standing beside her, his yellowish-white hair hanging down, soaked by the rain. He was looking up at her, smiling a worm-eaten smile.

'Perhaps I can be of service?' he said.

'And who are you, my man?' said Hanna Frankenstein.

'I am Igor,' said the hunchback, smiling his worm-eaten smile again. He tapped a bulge on the side of his neck with a dull bony sound.

'They tried to hang Igor when he was young, but Igor survived,' he said. 'Igor always survives.'

'And how old are you now, Igor?' said the old lady.

'I'm ninety-nine in February.'

'Then you were old in Henry's time,' said Hanna Frankenstein. 'So you're still alive, are you, you old joker?'

'Igor survives everything,' said Igor again. 'Can I be of service to you?'

'Well, why not?'

Hanna Frankenstein looked searchingly at the little hunchback. He had been a trifle unreliable in her nephew's time, muddling some vital organs and that kind of thing when they had been making the Monster. But perhaps he would be able to rustle up a cab. She told him to.

The worm-eaten smile appeared for the third time. Hanna Frankenstein decided that if she were going to have anything to do with Igor in the future, she would simply have to send him to a dentist.

'Igor has his own cab,' said Igor. 'Come with me.'

He gestured to her to follow him and limped away into the rain.

In the darkness behind the station was a haycart with large wheels, harnessed to a miserably thin old nag. Hanna Frankenstein could see the dripping ghost-like contours of the equipage in the light of the lamp.

'So you call that a cab, do you?' she said. 'A haycart!'

'That's no haycart, Madam,' said Igor with a smile. 'It's an old executioner's wagon. I bid for it for next to nothing at the auction, when the executioner in Ingold-stadt died a year or two back.'

'How practical,' said Hanna Frankenstein. 'And nice.'

Igor flung her cases up into the cart.

'Careful! Mind my sherry,' she said.

'Where to, Madam?'

Igor hauled himself up, surprisingly nimbly for his age, then stretched out a bony hand to her.

'Where do you think?' said Hanna Frankenstein, plumping herself down beside him on the wet hay.

As the cart got going, creaking and squealing, for a moment she had an unpleasant feeling of being on her way to her own execution, but she waved the thought away as imaginative nonsense, put up her umbrella and lit a cigar.

'What do things look like up there?' she said.

'Not too good. They blew up the laboratory. And the castle's in a bad way.'

'Oh, that Henry!' said his aunt. 'Making *one* Monster, that's just passable. But then to go and make a *bride* for the

14

Monster, too ... I think that's taking things rather too far.'

'Yes, that's what the villagers thought, too, but it was Dr Pretorius' idea,' said Igor.

'Yes, yes, I know all that, only too well,' said Hanna Frankenstein. 'I remember getting a letter from Henry saying how happy he was to have met Dr Pretorius ... and as usual, of course, he wanted to borrow money. Otherwise he never wrote. I wrote back at once, trying to warn him. "That Dr Pretorius seems to have several more screws loose than you have," I wrote. But Henry wouldn't listen, as usual. He was never one to heed warnings.'

'No, Dr Frankenstein was not a man to be afraid,' said Igor in a dreamy voice. 'That he wasn't.'

Hanna Frankenstein noticed the dreamy voice and grew irritable.

'Henry was not only unafraid,' she said in a loud voice. 'He was also terribly unwise, irresponsible and immature! He's always been the black sheep of the family.'

Igor cleared his throat and said more cautiously:

'How is he nowadays?'

'The last time I heard from him, he was thinking of emigrating to South America. But I hear he's still in some unknown place in Europe.'

'Isn't he thinking of coming back?'

'He's no doubt careful not to!' said Hanna Frankenstein. 'He's no doubt careful not to!'

It was easy to hear just *whom* Henry was careful not to come back to.

They had left the village now, the last houses disappearing into the darkness behind them.

The rain was pouring down harder than ever now. A great streak of lightning lit up the countryside, revealing that they were on their way up into the mountains. In the bluish-white light, Hanna Frankenstein could see the road winding its stony pot-holed way up ahead of the horse, between high cliffs and dense pine-forest. Right up at the top, crowning the wild scene, the castle suddenly came into view, illuminated by the next flash of lightning, a derelict ghostly fortress with dripping walls, the roof collapsed, ragged clouds chasing round it, the windows black as empty eye-sockets.

The Castle

They drove through a narrow ravine where tree roots reared out of the mud like gnarled hands. The screeching of the cart's crooked wheels, the glip-glop of hoofs in the mud, the splashing of the pouring rain and the almost incessant growl of thunder made all normal conversation quite impossible. They had to shout at each other, and Aunt Frankenstein had to shout the loudest, because Igor was slightly deaf.

'Is it possible to live up there at all?' she bawled.

'Igor lives there,' said Igor.

That was a surprise to Hanna Frankenstein, not altogether a pleasant surprise. She made a swift calculation in her head as to how much it would cost to send Igor to the dentist.

'Oh, so you still live there, do you, Igor? In what part of the castle, may I ask?'

'In the kitchen,' screeched Igor. 'It's warmest there.'

The next moment, the rain-whipped air was sliced in two by a terrible flash of lightning almost simultaneously with a tremendous clap of thunder. The horse reared up on its hind legs, neighing wildly, and Igor was only just able to stop it bolting. Aunt Frankenstein drew angrily on her cigar, which refused to burn properly in the rain, fierce raindrops coming right through her umbrella and falling like mist all over her. She was soon soaked through to the skin and longed to get indoors, but when she saw the ruined castle up there in the next flash of lightning, she wondered what 'indoors' would really mean.

Igor sensed her anxiety and croaked out a sound she supposed was meant to be a laugh. Hanna Frankenstein began to shiver all over. She could get furious with people who didn't give her a straight answer to her questions.

'Is it possible to live up there, or isn't it?' she snapped.

'Oh, well, you know,' said Igor. 'If you mend the windows and get a decent fire going, it's probably all right, I should think.'

He told Aunt Frankenstein that there were bats in the chandelier in what remained of the dining-room. So Hanna Frankenstein decided that it was no use being surprised by anything in future and, in an icy calm voice, said:

'And I suppose there are werewolves in the drawing-room?'

'No,' said Igor, who didn't understand plurals. 'I ain't seen him for ages. Maybe he's gone abroad, him too, like young Mr Henry, you know. And I ain't seen the Count for a while, neither.'

'The Count? What Count?'

'Count Dracula, of course,' said Igor, and Hanna Frankenstein's broad shoulders shuddered. She didn't like vampires, in fact disliked them as much as mosquitoes. The very thought of vampires flapping round her ears while she was eating her evening sandwich depressed her.

'Are you sure those bats in the dining-room aren't Count Dracula and his family?' she said. 'Perhaps he's been breeding.'

'Oh,' said Igor. 'I think I'd recognise the Count. No, them's just ordinary small bats, so there's no need to worry, Missis.'

'I'm *not* worrying,' said Aunt Frankenstein icily. 'I'm going to put things straight in that castle again, even if werewolves and vampires are queuing up in the hall!'

They arrived. The cart stopped with a jerk and the squeaking stopped too, the silence afterwards almost foreboding, the stone walls of the castle rising glistening wet out of the darkness. The thorny jungle of briars climbed high up the walls like greedy claws, the rain rustling down into the undergrowth.

'Looks as if Sleeping Beauty had slept here,' muttered Hanna Frankenstein, trying to light her cigar.

At that moment, another streak of forked lightning flashed across the sky, lighting up the collapsed roof of the castle. For a moment it looked like the cracked ribs of a giant dead lizard, a swarm of crows flapping away like frightened vultures, their croaks blending with the crash of thunder. Yet another flash of lightning and the castle glared down at Hanna Frankenstein with empty eyes edged with slivers of broken glass.

'It's nothing but a ruin,' said Aunt Frankenstein, somewhat subdued.

'I told you the windows needed mending!' screeched Igor, laughing in a nasty way Hanna Frankenstein thought quite unnecessary. She straightened up to her full height, picked up her bag containing the sherry and said in a steely voice: 'Igor! Show me the way. I wish to inspect this appalling mess.'

Igor unhooked the lantern, jumped down to the ground, held the lantern above his head and said from under his streaky wet fringe:

'Can I help you down, Missis?'

'I can manage quite well, thank you,' said Hanna

Frankenstein, angrily hitching up her skirts. When she put her boots down into a puddle, Igor sniggered.

'Missis, you're nearly as large as the Monster!' he said.

'Thank you very much,' said Aunt Frankenstein. 'I take that as a compliment.' She sounded like a talking lemon.

'I only meant your height,' said Igor cautiously.

'Yes, yes,' said Hanna Frankenstein. 'Don't worry. We probably take the same size shoes, too, the Monster and I. When I was a little girl and had to go for violin lessons when it was raining, I used to put my violin inside my boot. Hurry up now! I'm as wet as a drowned cat.'

Igor raised the lantern again and limped on ahead of her down a tunnel through the jungle of briars.

'We'll have to go the back way, if you'll excuse me, Missis,' he said. 'The front door's quite overgrown.'

The yellow light shone into the tangle of briars, raindrops glistening like sparkling wine. Hanna Frankenstein walked bent over double behind Igor, a giant lady following the bow-legged dwarf. The light fell on to a wet wooden door with rusty ironwork, and Igor turned round with another unappetising laugh.

'This is where I live,' he said with delight. 'Come in, come in.'

He pushed open the door. It opened with a great creaking into coal-black cellar darkness, the flickering light of the lantern apparently hesitating on the threshold.

'Come in, come in,' said Igor again. 'I'm sorry it ain't very tidy.'

Hanna Frankenstein stepped into the castle kitchen, where the old man lived among rubbish and cobwebs in such squalor that she froze with horror. The pile of bedding and blankets in a heap in front of the open fire was clearly his sleeping-place. She at once took out her notebook from her bag and wrote: *Things that must be got: For Igor: ordinary child's bed*. Then in brackets she wrote: (*Make an appointment with the dentist . . . for an estimate*).

She saw in the corner beyond the fire a spiral stone staircase winding up into the darkness. Igor told her it led up to the great entrance hall, then he shuffled ahead of her with the lantern, their shadows floating and swaying grotesquely over the stone walls.

The door into the great hall opened with a howling draught, the light from the lantern taking a feeble leap out into the damp darkness and being almost at once swallowed up by the size of the hall. The scene became even more frightening in the inadequate yellow light. Beyond the mildewed and partly fungus-covered wooden door were large shiny black puddles. In one corner was a rusted suit of armour, its perforated breastplate more like a brown skeleton than armour. In another corner, a rat was sitting staring in surprise, the yellow light reflected in its peppercorn eyes; and on both sides of the slimy green stone stairs leading up to the next floor, cobwebs were hanging down from the ceiling like dirty billowing grey draperies.

Aunt Frankenstein wrote down in her little book: *Feather dusters, ladder, scrubbing-bucket, broom, rat-traps, cheese, more sherry*.

Then she said:

'Igor! I presume there is an inn in the village. I will pay for you to stay the night there if you will drive me back. I have no intention of putting a foot inside this ghastly castle until my secretary comes. I'll send for him first thing tomorrow morning.'

Talk in
the Village Inn

It was some days later on a murky weekday evening in the village inn. The station-master put his glass down with a bang.

'Innkeeper! Another glass of sherry ... sweet, please.'

'Coming, Helmut!' said the innkeeper, shuffling over to the table with the bottle, his striped apron tight across his stomach, his face with its black moustache shining like a greasy sun. He drew the cork out with his great hairy hands and filled the station-master's glass. The guard, sitting at the same table, wiped the froth off his drooping yellowing moustache.

'Why can't you drink beer like the rest of us?' he said. 'Or at least our local wine?'

He had just come off duty from the night train to Munich, and he still had a red mark across his forehead from his peaked cap. They had walked up from the station together.

'I have my habits and you have yours,' the station-master said grumpily. '*If* I ever take a drink, then I drink sweet sherry. Full stop!'

His taste for sweet sherry was a fly in the ointment for more than one person and some people considered it womanish of him.

The innkeeper laughed good-naturedly.

'*If* you ever take a drink! Don't you come here every single evening?' He banged in the cork with his hairy fist and shuffled back behind the counter.

'Not the other evening,' said the station-master. 'I was working until long past midnight then.' He lowered his voice and peered cautiously to left and right. 'That was the evening *she* came.'

'Yes, I ought to have kicked her off the train as soon as I saw who she was. When I read her name on the ticket, I could feel my hair standing on end under my cap, that I could.'

'What's she doing here?' said the station-master. 'What does she want?'

'Don't you see?' said the guard. 'She's going to bring the Monster back to life, of course!'

'No, no, don't say that!' said the station-master, spilling a drop or two of sherry on his tie, his thin hands trembling.

The innkeeper came over to their table again, drying a glass so that it squeaked as he twisted the cloth inside the glass.

'I think you can take it easy, you two,' he said benignly. 'That night she stayed here in the inn ... well, I didn't want to let her have a room at first when I heard her name, but my Irmgard took pity on her. It was a terrible night and Irmgard's got a heart of gold ...'

'Otto!' someone called from the kitchen, and the innkeeper replied: 'Yes, dear heart?'

Irmgard, the innkeeper's wife, put her head into the taproom, her cheeks rosy-red from the stove.

'Otto, where's the cinnamon?' she said. 'I'm making apple-pies and I can't find the cinnamon.'

'It's next to the icing-sugar on the shelf above the stove,' said the innkeeper. 'But Irmgard, my treasure,

23

now you're here, can't you come over and tell Helmut and Fritz what old Aunt Frankenstein said to you the other evening?'

Irmgard came into the taproom, the smell of apples swirling in with her skirts. She was a large woman with long fair plaits and a bosom like two round loaves. She blew a strand of hair away from her rosy face and said: 'It sounded to me as if she had come here to tidy up the castle a bit and clean up the family's reputation.'

'Well, both those are very much needed, indeed they are,' said the guard, froth on his moustache.

'That's what it sounded like to me,' said Irmgard.

'Do you hear what she says, you two?' said the innkeeper. 'But don't let's hold you up, my dear. You just go on out to your apple-pies again.'

The innkeeper and his wife exchanged a loving look before she retreated back into the warmth of her stove. Although they had been married for twenty years, every evening they behaved as if they had just fallen in love.

'That secretary she's sent for, what sort of drip is he?' said the station-master suspiciously, hunching over his sherry.

'Don't ask me,' said the guard. 'I was off duty when he came.'

The innkeeper gave the glass one last polish and held it up to the light.

'A pale thin little wretch of about thirty,' he said. 'A typical intellectual. Glasses. Briefcase. He should have stayed here with Mother Irmgard and me for a few days to feed himself up a bit. He had a bad cold, too.'

The Castle Kitchen, the Same Evening

'Well, Frans,' said Hanna Frankenstein. 'Now you've seen what it looks like. What do you think?'

They were sitting with Igor in the kitchen after a second very thorough tour of the castle. A wood fire was roaring in the fireplace and Igor was standing hunched over it, stirring honey into boiling water in a sooty copper pan, their shadows fluttering hugely over the floor and walls.

'Not a pleasant sight,' said Frans.

He pushed his glasses up with a thin hand and jerked his stool a little closer to the fire. He had a huge red scarf wound several times round his neck and, against the red wool, his thin face looked almost transparently pale, like candle-grease or cheap soap. His reddish hair was thin and fluffed up and his nickel-framed glasses kept slipping down, the thick lenses misted and thumb-marked, giving the impression he could see over them better than through them.

'Mr Frans,' said Igor. 'Would you like some honey-water?'

He came hobbling over with a steaming tin mug.

'Thank you, Igor, very good of you,' said Frans, cautiously accepting the scalding tin mug. 'And please stop calling me Mr, Igor. Just say Frans. That's enough.'

'Missis Frankenstein?' said Igor, shuffling up to Aunt Frankenstein, who was sitting with her knees apart, leaning forward on a tiny stool and smoking a cigar. 'Would you like some honey-water, Missis Frankenstein?'

'Thanks, I'll stick to sherry,' she said, twirling her glass round. 'And may I take this opportunity of requesting you to call me Aunt instead of Missis? I don't like all this bowing and scraping. No cringing in my house, if you please. I can't stand that.'

'Certainly Missis,' said Igor, bowing several times. 'I mean, Aunt Frankenstein.'

'Good honey-water,' said Frans. 'Very good indeed.' He blew on his steaming mug.

'Well,' said Hanna Frankenstein. 'What do you think?'

'It'll be a terrible job,' said Frans. 'No doubt about that.'

He still had a picture of the derelict dining-room at the back of his mind, and he shuddered as he thought of it. It had been a cloudy morning when he had first gone in there, and a gloomy grey light had trickled down through the shattered windows in the roof. Baron Frankenstein, deceased, Henry's father and Hanna's brother, had been an original man, and he had chosen to have his dining-room on the upper floor so that he could have his dinner beneath the sky all the year round. But now the windows had been in ruins for many years and the rain and wind had sat at the table with very bad table manners. The once beautiful room was now totally ruined, with cracked panelling and rotting floorboards, and there were bats hanging asleep like black pears in the rusting remains of the chandelier. On their second visit, which they had made that evening, the bats had been woken by Igor's lantern and had swooped round their ears with wings that looked like small brown umbrellas against the light.

Frans shivered again and took a swallow of honey-water, forgetting to blow this time and burning his tongue.

'There's no doubt the castle is in a disgraceful condition,' he said. 'Pah!' He touched the tip of his tongue.

'Cleaning the place up would . . .' said Hanna Frankenstein, and they could almost hear the great gloomy void at the end of the sentence.

'Is the laboratory in the same appalling state?' said Frans, blowing his nose.

'The laboratory?' Hanna Frankenstein sat bolt upright on her stool. 'Igor! You never showed us the laboratory!'

'Oh, that. There's nothing much to see,' said Igor evasively. 'Mr Frans, would you like a little more honey-water?'

Aunt Frankenstein had risen to her full height and her now warm boots creaked as she steered a course for Igor. He saw that this was no time for honey-water and hurriedly picked up his lantern.

'This way,' he whimpered, hobbling up the stairs. 'But there's not much to see . . .'

At the
Village Inn Again

The station-master sipped his sherry.

'I'll have you know I've found it hard to sleep at nights since *she* came,' he said. 'Ever since, there's been lights showing up there in the castle, that's been the end of my beauty sleep. Same for the wife, too.'

The innkeeper absent-mindedly wiped the table with his cloth, although he had only just done it, and the guard was given yet another opportunity to lift his beer-mat.

'I've only seen lights on in the actual castle,' said the innkeeper. 'It's been just as dark in the laboratory as before. And you heard what Irmgard said, that it sounded as if she's only come to clean up the castle and the family name a little.'

'Well, I've got my own ideas about that,' said the guard, wiping the froth off his moustache. 'I spied on her a bit out in the corridor, that night on the train, and with my own eyes I saw her sitting there with that fat yellow old tome ... and on one occasion she sort of raised her hands in front of her like ... well, you know who I mean!'

'Mark my words, she was reading the instructions,' said the station-master in a hollow voice. 'Yes, you mark my words, things are getting like the old days again.' He lowered his voice and looked round. 'And you know

what? I met the post-mistress yesterday. She'd been picking harebells and, when she was on her way home, she
thought she saw a man rather like that Talbot on the edge
of the forest!'

'Talbot!' said the innkeeper. 'You mean that American
who ...'

He had no wish to mention the evil creature by name.

'But he hasn't been seen around here for years!'

'Yes, that's what I was saying. It's beginning to look
like the old days again. And it'll soon be full moon.' He
raised his glass to take a sip of sherry, but stopped in the
middle of the movement and turned deathly pale.
Through the inn window, which was slightly open to let
out the tobacco smoke, they heard a distant long drawn-
out howl, rising and falling, echoing through the village
streets in the spring evening.

'Did you hear that?' he hissed.

'Only a dog,' said the innkeeper uncertainly. 'Old man
Meyer's dog, as usual.'

'Meyer's not at home,' said the guard. 'He's gone to see
his sister in Neuburg.'

'Well, that's probably why the dog's howling, then,'
said the innkeeper. 'You can't mean it ... no, I can't
believe it.' He shuffled over to the taproom counter to
fetch the sherry bottle. 'On the house, Helmut,' he said.

He filled the deathly-pale station-master's glass and
then eased his way past the table to close the window.

'Pity I don't drink sherry,' mumbled the guard into his
empty beer tankard.

The innkeeper was standing with his stomach pressed
against the window-niche, staring out into the blue April
night. At the end of the village street, he could see the
mist lying white over the valley, and on the other side of
the valley rose the dark mountains. A pale almost full

moon was shining down on to Frankenstein Castle up there. But the moon wasn't the only light he could see.

'Listen, men!' he said over his shoulder, and his voice was suddenly hoarse. *'There's a light on in the laboratory now!'*

A Surprise in the Laboratory

It was built as an annexe to the castle, in shape more like the central stem of an old-fashioned windmill or a tall wheat-silo. It was built of stone and had only a few tiny little slits of windows in its thick walls. Its tower-like interior was filled to the brim with complicated chemical and electrical apparatus climbing and coiling up the walls, and a free space ran up the middle, filled with a lift-arrangement of chains and cables right up to the great hatches in the roof.

Unlike the castle, the electric light was still working here. Igor had pulled a huge switch just inside the door and bluish-white light had blazed down on to them from four searchlight-like lamps rigged up among the apparatus. Hanna Frankenstein felt as if she were on a stage as she made her entrance into the heap of rubble, and for a dizzy moment she turned sentimental. In her youth, she had always wanted to go on the stage but had been prevented by her mother, who considered her too tall, her nose too big and her feet too large.

She looked round. The devastation in the laboratory was far less great than in the castle itself. Stones that had fallen after the unsuccessful attempt to blow the place up lay all over the floor, but all the laboratory equipment looked more or less undamaged. She pushed aside a few stones with her boot, took a step back and looked up at the glittering confusion of spiral glass tubes, thermometer-like objects, cables, wires and great globes of glass. She shaded her eyes with her hand and took another step back, and as she did so she knocked against a glass jar on the edge of a crowded table. It fell to the ground with a small crash.

Frans bent down to look at the broken pieces.

'It was empty,' he said.

'That's just what happened,' said Igor, peering up at Aunt Frankenstein. 'That's just what happened when I went to fetch that brain, though the jar wasn't empty, of course.'

'*Fetch*?' said Hanna Frankenstein. 'Had you *ordered* a brain?' she went on, pretending she didn't know the procedure, although she knew perfectly well, as she had read in Henry's notes all about the distasteful way they had collected material for the Monster.

Igor wriggled and blinked.

'Well, no, I mean, I broke in, of course ... at night ... into the Pathological Institute in Ingolstadt. But that was on Mr Henry's express orders. A famous brain surgeon had just finished a lecture on the structure of the brain. All the students had gone, and it was dark in the lecture-hall. Just as I was about to take the jar Mr Henry had described to me ...'

'The one containing the brain of a deceased and very famous scientist?' said Hanna Frankenstein.

'Yes, quite, yes ... him. The weather was terrible that night, and just as I was going to take the jar, a great flash of lightning struck and I jumped ... and there was the jar lying broken on the floor. So I was forced to grab the next best jar I could lay my hands on.'

'And that happened to be a jar containing a rather less famous brain,' said Aunt Frankenstein icily. 'Yes, I've read Henry's notes. But you never *said* anything when you came back with the wrong brain ... with very aggravating results for Henry. And for the villagers.'

'Oh, Missis,' said Igor, wriggling with torment. 'Aunt, dear, please don't let's talk about that any more. It was an accident at work.'

Hanna Frankenstein gave him a dark look and lit up a cigar.

'I think you could at least have told me the laboratory was in such reasonable condition. I could have lived here. At least it's dry underfoot.'

'Well, you see,' said Igor. 'I don't really *like* it much in here.'

'I think it's rather nice,' said Frans, stepping among the stones. 'I'd like to take a slightly closer look at these things.'

He looked up at the electrical apparatus, blew on his hands and beat his arms round him, suddenly much more cheerful.

'Where does that door lead to?'

He was pointing into a dark corner and looking at Aunt Frankenstein and Igor over the top of his glasses, his breath rising in a cloud above his scarf in the bright light. It was cold in there.

'Nowhere!' said Igor, leaping forward on his bandy legs. 'Nowhere!'

He placed himself in front of the door as if trying to hide it from their gaze.

Hanna Frankenstein smelt a rat at once and went across to him. The old man was trying to hide a rusty iron door. She pointed her long bony finger at him. 'What's this door?'

'You can't open it,' said Igor swiftly.

'Can't you? Where does it go to?'

'Nowhere! Nowhere!'

'Did you hear, Frans?' said Hanna Frankenstein. 'A door leading to Nowhere. That sounds fascinating. Pure metaphysics. Move over, Igor.'

Igor heard from her tone of voice it was no good resisting, so he turned away from the door with a helpless whimpering sound, and Aunt Frankenstein grasped the rusty key with both her large hands. With a grating squeal, the door opened and a puff of damp earthy air mixed with a strange sweetness billowed out at them. Aunt Frankenstein stared down the narrow stone stairway that twisted away into the darkness. There was a smell of apples and mulched leaves, rather like a game-store . . . or what was it?

'Aha!' she said. 'I've found the wine-cellar. That's why you didn't want me to open it, is it, you rascal?'

'No, no,' said Igor. 'That's not why at all.'

'Give me the lantern!' said Aunt Frankenstein, taking it from him, then saying to Frans. 'Hold the door open so that I get some light from above.'

She gathered her skirts up in her other hand, crouched and started down the narrow stairs. The stones were slippery and green, like steps down to a boat on a quay where the tide ebbs and flows over them, and she had to put her feet down with the greatest of care. She heard Igor call from behind her: 'Missis Frankenstein, dear Missis, you really oughtn't.'

The peculiar smell grew stronger. Was it smoked lamb? Or salami sausages? And then that sweet smell? Apple-rings? Dried apricots? Something else, too. Sour milk? Yoghurt? No, yoghurt had no smell. She went on down, one step at a time. It was cold down there, icy cold, her breath standing out round her in a cloud, glittering in all the colours of the rainbow in the light from the lantern. Or was it cigar-smoke? No, she had handed her cigar to Frans, because she had thought there just might be inflammable substances down there. She noticed she was slightly tense.

The yellow circle of light fell on to a pile of stones at the foot of the stairs. She saw a stone-walled vault with stalactites hanging from the roof, and she heard the drops falling first on to stone, then on to water, spitt ... spitt ... plop! Thin sounds, but quite different in character. It was as silent as a tomb.

She stopped, crouched over a pile of stones and raised the lantern.

A tomb ...

What was that sticking out from under the stones?

A foot.

A very large foot. Actually slightly larger than her own. A muddy boot with a very thick sole. A leg, a black trouser-leg. Might be serge. She started shifting stones aside, the smell of game-store getting stronger. She took stones away from the edge of the heap. A hand became visible, two metres from the foot. It was not beautiful. She put the stone back.

As she did that, she happened to start a minor avalanche, small stones bringing with them large ones and, in a cloud of dust, the heap of stones fell apart. And there! When the dust had settled, there lay the head Henry had described in his notes! She knew that passage off by heart by now: *And the head I had worked so hard on! I had tried to give him a high intellectual forehead, and the forehead was high enough, but far too high, and his hair hung down in black straggles from the flat skull ...*

The Monster was lying there in a peaceful torpor, smelling of smoked lamb and dried apricots.

She felt almost solemn.

A Slumbering Prince

'Now listen to what I've got to say!'

Hanna Frankenstein was standing with her feet apart in the castle kitchen, the wood fire burning behind her, throwing her shadow far out on to the floor. She was looking larger than usual.

'Igor is an old man, and Frans, you've only got muscles for desk-work. Nothing wrong with that. You've many good points, and you know I think so. I have never complained. But we're not going to be able to manage this on our own. You've seen the state the castle is in. The roof must be mended and every room gone through ... and the garden's a jungle.'

'Yes, but Aunt Frankenstein, my dear,' said Frans. 'The risks!'

'I am quite aware of the risks involved,' said Hanna Frankenstein. 'But we will only have him as a carpenter and handyman. I could see he was a strong creature. Heavens above, what hands! Like lavatory lids.'

'Yes, his left hand comes from a lumberjack in Neuburg,' said Igor. 'And if I remember rightly, a butcher in Himmelsdorff gave ...'

'*Silence!*' cried Aunt Frankenstein. 'I do not wish to hear another word about where the raw materials came from. That spoils the whole sculptural experience.'

'You don't mean you think he's beautiful, do you, Aunt Frankenstein?' said Frans in disbelief.

'Not beautiful, but powerful. And there's something

peaceful about him, like a sleeping child. Something innocent. Something pure. No decay at all. On the contrary. He was lying there like a slumbering prince.'

'Powerful, peaceful, innocent, prince!' said Frans. 'Are we really talking about the Monster?'

'Yes, we're talking about the Monster,' said Hanna Frankenstein. 'And I'm sure he was much misunderstood. I'm sure he never had a chance to show who he really was.'

'*Which* he really was,' said Igor. 'Because he consists of parts from at least eight . . .'

'SILENCE!' cried Aunt Frankenstein again. 'Can't you keep quiet about that? Can't you keep it a professional secret?'

'By all means,' said Igor rather huffily. 'I won't trouble you with it. But I was wrong about his right hand. It came from a dried-fruit merchant from Bremen. But I shan't trouble you with it.'

'Well, then,' said Hanna Frankenstein. 'I am fully aware of the risks. But I think it would be a great pity if we didn't use such an untapped source of energy. As soon as the job's done, we can put him to sleep again.'

She drew on her cigar and flicked the ash into the fire. Frans looked doubtfully up at her from where he was sitting.

'Well, I'm not having anything to do with it,' he said, pushing up his glasses. 'You'll have to take the responsibility, Aunt.'

'At last!' she said. 'Now, Igor, answer me! Do you know what to do to wake him up again?'

'Yes, I know,' said Igor. 'But I'm not going to tell you. I won't trouble you with it.'

The Prince Awakens

It was a damp night with low clouds racing across the sky, the thunder rumbling but still in the distance. Lightning lit up the whole sky with a flashing breathless blue light, the claps of thunder apparently coming from on high and then in long cracking tumbling waves descending into a rumbling mumbling rolling on the horizon, the rain pouring down, rustling and rattling in the undergrowth round the castle. A sharp bluish-white light shone out of the narrow windows in the laboratory tower.

A soaking wet raven had sought shelter from the rain in one of the topmost windows and was tramping up and down on his ice-cold feet, fluffing out his feathers and peering in through the window. Far away down there in the stone well, he could see one black and two white figures moving round a fourth figure lying on some kind of bunk. The fourth figure looked like one of those two-legged creatures being carried home from battle. The raven was very old and had flown over many a battlefield in his day. Nowadays he could no longer be bothered with two-legged creatures and their strange activities. He turned his back on them, hunched up and fell into a raven-black slumber.

Inside the laboratory, Hanna Frankenstein looked up at the hatch in the roof. The rain was rattling against the metal plates, and another flash of lightning flickered through the windows . . . she thought she saw a large bird perched in one of them.

'What terrible weather,' she said, an unlit cigar in the corner of her mouth.

'Just as it should be!' said Igor. 'Just as it should be!'

'It's coming closer,' said Frans, sitting with a pair of earphones on, staring at the flickering needle of a gauge.

'It'll soon be time to send up the kites,' said Igor delightedly.

Igor and Frans were wearing white coats tied at the back – Igor's idea, because, as he said, that was as it should be. He had tried to get a white coat on to Aunt Frankenstein, too, but she had refused to have anything to do with such nonsense. She thought her sturdy black travelling costume was perfectly adequate for the matter in question.

The Monster, or The Prince, as Frans insisted on calling him, was lying on his back on a high bunk rather like an operating table, his arms down his sides, his body bandaged from head to foot. Hanna Frankenstein did not know what the bandages were for, but presumed things would be different when 'the boy was re-made', as she called it, but Igor insisted that everything was as it should be. She made no objections, as it was not worth arguing about. Perhaps the Monster kept himself warmer that way during the warming-up process.

She lit her cigar and looked round the laboratory walls. Frans and Igor had done all the necessary repairs in there in three days. She herself had spent the time trying to tidy up two fairly undamaged bedrooms in the castle, as well as Henry's library. By having a roaring fire in the tiled stoves she had actually made the bedrooms habitable, and there was hope for the library . . . at least she could have her glass of sherry there in the evenings. Soon she would have some help with the repairs to the rest of the castle. She looked expectantly at the bandaged giant and felt like a little girl at Christmas, impatiently waiting for the hours to go by before she could open her parcels.

'Well, boys,' she said. 'What are we waiting for?'

Frans had taken off the earphones.

'We're waiting for the thunder to come directly overhead,' he said. 'It'll be here any moment now.'

After the repair work had been completed, they had had to wait for three more days for suitable weather.

Technically and scientifically-minded as Frans was, he had soon familiarised himself with the whole procedure, for which Aunt Frankenstein was extremely grateful because, when it came to electricity, she herself was quite ignorant and she didn't entirely trust Igor.

Frans leant over the Monster, rather like a short-sighted surgeon bending over his patient. A short little metal rod protruded from the bandages on each side of the Monster's neck, and to these rods Frans coupled cables hanging down from the roof. As he fastened the cable-ends down, Aunt Frankenstein said:

'So the current will go through those hinges in his neck, will it? I understand that much.'

'They're not hinges,' said Igor haughtily. 'That's the cathode and that's the anode,' he went on, pronouncing both words in grandiose scientific tones.

'Like the poles in a battery,' said Frans, without a glimmer of superiority, the quality in him Aunt Frankenstein appreciated most of all.

Frans pointed:

'Plus on this side of the neck, and minus on that side.'

At that moment, a blinding flash of lightning whistled through the laboratory and the clap of thunder followed almost immediately, shaking and rattling the hatch as if from a violent whirlwind.

'The time's come!' shouted Igor. 'Open the hatches!'

Frans reached out towards the switch. The hum of an engine could be heard somewhere, then a piercing screech as the rusty hatches in the roof slid apart. Down came the rain in gusts, extinguishing Aunt Frankenstein's cigar with a bull's eye as she stood there with her face turned upwards. Ragged clouds were racing past the open hatch and another flash of lightning turned them as white as torn sails. The laboratory was filled with the raging thunderstorm, howling wildly like a ghostly organ through the spiral glass tubes and shiny steel rods. Their hair was tossed wildly in the wind, Aunt Frankenstein's iron grey locks, Igor's yellowish tufts, and Frans's reddish-fair fluff which suddenly turned into a dramatic shock of hair.

'Switch on!' shouted Igor.

Hanna Frankenstein suddenly felt she must take part in the performance. She wanted to play a major part, and it was no use just standing in the wings any longer.

'Let me! Let me!' she cried, leaping forward.

Frans was already prepared to pull down the huge switch, but he immediately relinquished the rôle. Aunt Frankenstein grasped the worn wooden handle, closed her eyes and . . . pulled!

Long crackling snaky strips of light began to curl up the tall glass tubes round the walls, then the whole apparatus started vibrating and glowing red, orange and blue.

'Up with the kites!' yelled Igor, who wished to be the producer of the play. 'Up with the table! Press that button there!'

Frans glanced at him rather irritably. He had read it all up carefully and knew what to do . . . and Igor knew that he knew, too. They loosened a row of moorings and, up from the laboratory floor, four box-shaped sailcloth kites rose into the wind. These kites had been specially made by Henry Frankenstein and his colleague Dr Pretorius: to trap the hitherto unknown kind of electricity that was released in violent thunderstorms and contained the life-giving sparks that reversed all known theories on electricity. The kites rose up into the racing clouds, their ropes shining with a green phosphorescent light.

Down on the floor, the needles on the control panel were rocking violently, and the time had come to elevate the table with the Monster on it. Frans turned on another switch and, with a piercing clattering screech, the table rose into the sky on its four chains. Up through the stone well of the laboratory slid the Monster, through an inferno of flashing arcs of light and vibrating orange and blueish-white light. Aunt Frankenstein had been standing at the end of the table, and she watched the soles of the great boots ascending higher and higher, illuminated by the flickering light.

'Good luck, Frankie Boy!' she cried. 'And come down human, God and all the fuses willing!'

In the middle of all the excitement, she noticed that one of the boots needed soling.

Frans was following the ascent of the Monster on the control panel, the needles violently swinging back and forth, plunging far too often into the red area marked danger.

'The tension's terrific!' he cried.

'Yes, it certainly is!' yelled Aunt Frankenstein in reply. 'I'm beginning to understand Henry.'

'I don't mean that sort of tension!' shouted Frans. 'Electric tension . . . the voltage!'

DANGER! screamed all his instruments. Cold sweat broke out on his forehead, his glasses falling right down to the tip of his nose and his hair standing on end.

The thunderstorm had now reached a climax, lightning continually flashing above the roof, the Monster stretched out on his bunk on a level with the hatch up there, fully exposed to the mysterious life-giving forces. The thunder growled and roared and the floor shook, the whole laboratory apparently filling with electricity and the smell of phosphorous and burning bakelite.

Suddenly all the meter needles leapt into the red and fell back all at the same time. Frans crouched down. With a tremendous crack, an overloaded part of the apparatus exploded above his head, splinters of glass raining down all over the floor, and the laboratory filled with thick choking smoke.

'Let the table down again!' screamed Igor in a falsetto. 'Let it down, let it down!'

'Let it down yourself!' coughed Frans. 'I can't see my hand in front of my nose.'

'I hope that was the right button,' said Hanna Frankenstein.

She had already pressed a button she had found in the smoke, a button she thought had DOWN on it.

A great silence descended after the explosion. The thunder seemed to retreat and the storm abated. Gentle rain was falling on to the stone floor, slowly dispelling the smoke and, there in the yellowish mist, they saw the table come wafting down from above, like a bucket in a well of muddy water seen from the viewpoint of a frog, the chains creaking quietly.

With a tinkling thump, the table landed in the broken glass. Steam was coming out of the Monster, like from a freshly baked loaf. Hanna Frankenstein again noticed the smell of smoked lamb, sharper now, and mixed with a peculiar electric smell. Igor came hobbling through the broken glass, which crunched under his feet.

'Take the bandages off!' he squeaked.

Hanna Frankenstein had already started opening her parcel. The moment had come at last! As she unwound the bandages, she remembered almost word for word the lines in Henry's notes:

How can I describe my feelings as the bandages fell away and he finally opened his eyes? I had tried to give him a high intellectual forehead, and the forehead was high enough all right, but far too high, and his hair was hanging down in black straggles from his flat skull. But he was breathing. He was alive . . . !

'Good morning, Your Highness,' said Frans.

The Monster's watery eyes flickered, the eyelashes trembling. The puckered, still steaming skin of his face twitched, and his thin black lips stretched as he opened his mouth in a grimace. A dry whimper came out of his still bandaged chest, his lungs making a sound like the first breeze of spring rustling in last year's dead leaves . . .

Anxiety Spreads

The spring sunshine shone down on to the tiled and turf roofs, the gardens brilliant with broom and daffodils but, inside the village inn, the atmosphere was gloomy. A little group of men was gathered round the station-master as, hollow-eyed and thin, he spread anxiety in wider and wider circles.

'Now don't you go telling me they're just cleaning up that laboratory!' he said to the innkeeper, who was grumpily drying glasses at the counter. 'That light you can see up there at night, I recognise it . . . arc lights and blue flashes, just like in the old days!'

'But there was a terrible thunderstorm last night,' said the innkeeper.

'Do you think I can't tell the difference between God's lightning and Frankenstein's?' said the station-master. 'I'm telling you, men, I'm off home to pack my trunks. I'm leaving!'

'Now don't go doing anything rash, Helmut,' said Meyer, the auctioneer. He had just done his unpacking, as he had just come back on the night train from staying with his sister in Neuburg. Meyer was a stout elderly man with a walrus moustache and a bowler hat. He was leaning on his stick, a tankard of beer in his hand, and a weary old bulldog was sitting at his feet, as if it had not had much sleep on the train.

'We shouldn't think the worst,' said the village black-smith, a blue-eyed young man with short fair hair and arms like a bear's, his tankard of beer nestling like an egg-cup in his huge hand.

'I think Helmut's right,' said the guard, wiping the froth off his moustache. He had been on duty on the train Meyer had come on, and he was now off duty for the rest of the day, so was wearing sporting plus-fours and a Tyrolean hat.

'Well, something fishy's up. I think so, too,' said Muller the butcher, a huge man with a scarlet face and four double chins.

'You can say that again,' said the station-master.

At that moment, they all felt a draught in the room, the door behind the counter banged and, his cloth over his shoulder, the innkeeper went out into the kitchen. His customers could hear him talking to his wife out there. She had clearly just come in from out of doors, and her voice was loud and shrill. When the innkeeper came back into the taproom his face was as white as the cloth he had in his hand.

'What's the matter?' said the station-master. 'Why are you so pale?'

'Irmgard has just been out for a while looking for harebells . . .' said the innkeeper.

'Well . . .????' chorused his customers.

'And she happened to stray up towards the castle. She's . . . she's seen the Monster! It's going round up there tearing up bushes like a maniac!'

'*What did I tell you*?' said the station-master hoarsely.

The guard had by now drunk quite a number of tankards of beer. He pulled down his waistcoat and hitched up his plus-fours, the fear inside him subsiding.

'We must look into this,' he said in a determined voice. 'In good time, this time. Anyone coming up with me?'

'I've promised the brewer's drayman I'd shoe his

horses today,' said the blacksmith, hastily drinking up and leaving.

'And I've got some sausages to make for Mrs Braun,' said the butcher, following suit.

The guard straightened his Tyrolean hat and looked cheerfully at the remainder, suddenly feeling he was a born leader.

'You'll come, anyhow, won't you, Helmut?' he said. 'And you, Innkeeper? Can we borrow your hound, Meyer?'

'By all means,' said Meyer, handing over the lead. 'But he doesn't like walking uphill.'

The bulldog had fallen asleep in the sawdust on the inn floor.

Monster's First Day

The spring sun shone down on to the grey walls of the castle. Deep in the shadows of the tangle of briars, a huge figure was wrestling among the thorns, his movements stiff and uncertain, and a dull dissatisfied growling coming out of his throat. Now and again, he raised his hands and covered his face with fumbling helpless gestures to protect it from the sun and, when he did that, the black sleeves of his outgrown jacket slid back, revealing the great stitches in his wrists. His eyes were half-closed, his mouth half-open, his hair hanging down from his flat skull like grass over the edge of a cliff, the cathode and anode glinting in his neck in the spring sunlight. He grasped the bushes again with his great hands and heaved and hauled, pricking himself on the thorns and whimpering like a puppy.

'How're things going, Frankie?'

Aunt Frankenstein had come out of the kitchen door and was standing beside him. Although she was considered a large lady at one metre eighty-seven in her socks, she hardly reached his shoulder.

Monster looked down at her through lowered eyelids, fumbling with his hands with helpless gestures that became even more helpless in that jacket, and groaned miserably.

'I think I understand,' said Hanna Frankenstein. 'You think it's hard work, don't you? Well, perhaps it is a bit much putting you to clearing this jungle all at once.

You must be a bit weak after lying in a trance for so long.'

She took her cigar case out of her jacket pocket, fished out a large dark brown Brazilian cigar and put it in her mouth. Monster struggled to fix his watery yellow eyes on her and a glimmer of interest appeared in the flickering pupils.

'Yes, keep on looking,' said Aunt Frankenstein. 'Can you say *cigar*?'

Monster's mouth twitched and he put his large flat head slightly on one side. The cathode glinted, or maybe it was the anode. 'Arrr,' he said, both his black tongue and his voice resembling a parrot's.

'Say it again,' said Aunt Frankenstein. 'Ci – gar.'

Monster repeated it.

'Ci – garrr.'

A grin of happiness twisted the corners of his mouth upwards.

'There, you see?' said Aunt Frankenstein. 'You can say it. You used to be able to say whole sentences, so you'll have to start getting into training again.'

Monster repeated the word again, smiling happily. But suddenly his face went rigid with terror. He growled and took a stumbling step backwards, raising his hands to protect himself. Aunt Frankenstein had struck a match.

'Of course, dash it!' she said. 'You're afraid of fire, aren't you?' Quickly she blew out the match. 'There, there, it's all right. I'll smoke later.'

She put the matches back into her pocket again.

Monster took a step forward, fumbling miserably with his hands again.

'Ci – gar,' he said hesitantly, trying to make contact.

He took another stiff step forwards and came out into an open glade in the undergrowth. The sun fell on to his flat head and straight into his light-shy eyes. He growled angrily and struck out at the sun . . . there was something touchingly helpless about this colossal figure still only one day old in his new life, and Aunt Frankenstein thought perhaps even a monster should have his period of infancy.

'Listen, my friend,' she said. 'I'm sure you need a spell of convalescence before we can put you to work. I realise that now. You can take it easy for a few days.'

She bent down and picked a harebell she had seen in among the dead leaves. She gave it to Monster and said: 'Perhaps you could go and see if you can find any more of these for me?'

Monster looked at the harebell. It seemed minutely small in his giant yellow fingers.

'Ci – gar?' he said hesitantly, looking at Aunt Frankenstein.

'No, that's not a cigar,' she said. 'It's a *harebell*. Go and look for harebells now, and I'll go and see if I can do something about the sunlight for you. I think I saw an old straw hat in the toolshed.'

She made her way through the undergrowth, sucking on her unlit cigar.

Monster looked at the flower, holding it right up to his eyes.

'Hairy-bell,' he said, smiling broadly.

A few kilometres away, an observation patrol was on its way up the hill.

The Leader

The bulldog collapsed on to the sawdust at its master's feet and put its drooping cheeks on its paws. He had had a most frightful afternoon, filled with endless trudging up hills, the scents of sweat and frightened people, and he had seen and heard a whole lot of peculiar things he couldn't be bothered to think about now. He was snoring heavily before the conversation round the bar counter even started.

'We've seen enough!' said the guard, fanning his red face with his Tyrolean hat. 'Irmgard, my dear, a beer before I die!'

'Have you seen the Monster?' said the blacksmith, now finished with the drayman's horses.

'I'll say we've seen him!' said the guard, winking at Irmgard as she drew their beer, her blonde plaits dangling. He meant they had a horrible experience in common, but she misunderstood him and flushed deeply.

'What did he look like?' said the butcher, now finished with his sausages.

'Just as awful as usual,' said the guard, putting his tankard to his mouth. '*Worse* than usual,' he added, as he dipped his moustache into the beer.

The crush in the inn was enormous. Every single villager seemed to have come to hear what the three heroes had to say. The guard had now taken on the part of leader to them all, and it could be seen that he had taken the responsibility for the whole future of the village on to his

51

shoulders. As he had sloping shoulders, he seemed to be afraid the responsibility might slip off them at any moment.

'If I may state my opinion,' said the innkeeper, leaning against the counter, rosy-faced and sweaty, 'then I didn't think he looked all that dangerous. Not as I had expected.'

He at once received an angry look from the guard.

'What do you mean? Are you making light of the deadly danger threatening us all?'

'He was only going round in a straw hat picking harebells,' said the innkeeper.

A surprised hum ran round the inn, but the guard immediately demanded silence.

'*I*'m not deceived,' he said. 'You must see that's a trick. You must see that the old girl's trying to lull us into security.'

'Yes, Fritz is right,' said the station-master. 'I think it's a trick, too.'

'Was he really wearing a straw hat?' said old man Meyer.

'Yes,' said the innkeeper. 'He looked as peaceful as any gardener.'

'Some gardener!' said the guard loudly, so that he could be heard by everyone. 'A gardener just waiting to harvest the flowers of death.'

He thought he had found a really descriptive image and saw with pride that it had gone home. His words were received with dark and frightened looks. He was almost moved as he sensed this response in the villagers and he realised that he would now have to do everything to live up to their expectations. He asked Irmgard for another tankard of beer and said loudly:

'Tomorrow evening . . .' and then paused for effect.

'Tomorrow evening, we will form a posse. With dogs and torches.'

The bulldog raised one ear in its sleep, thinking some-one had mentioned him.

Larry Talbot Appears

It was lunch-time the following day.

Aunt Frankenstein was in the castle kitchen, feeding Monster with oatmeal porridge. Nothing seemed to have gone right with his resuscitation. Instead of gathering strength, he seemed to be getting weaker. Aunt Frankenstein was now desperately trying out a nourishing and digestible diet, but Monster did not seem to be appreciating her painstaking efforts. He was as whiny and grumpy as a difficult child and behaved very badly at table. Aunt Frankenstein could feel her patience giving out.

'Now a spoonful for Igor,' she said. 'You must eat so that you're strong enough to help repair the castle. We'll have to eat here in the kitchen until you've mended the roof in the dining-room.'

It was not a cheering thought. The kitchen was a squalid mess, a fly buzzing on the dirty window, some dry crusts and a sweaty piece of cheese lying in the niche below it. She hadn't immediately been able to do anything about Igor's bohemian bachelor habits. Aunt Frankenstein began to wonder what on earth she had let herself in for. Sitting in a gloomy kitchen in a ruined castle feeding a refractory monster with porridge was not what she had expected when she had set off from home.

She tried another spoonful, but Monster growled crossly, waving a great ham fist, and the whole lot fell on to the table.

'Oh, you clumsy great thing!' said Hanna Frankenstein. 'You should be in a baby-chair with counting-
beads.'

The thought went through her mind that it would be
the largest baby-chair in the whole world, but when she
saw the grimace of misery flit across Monster's face, she
patted him comfortingly on the hand and said: 'We'll see
how it goes. We'll see how it goes.'

They heard steps on the stairs and Frans came in.

'Aunt,' he said. 'There's a man up there in the hall
who's come to see you. He says his name is Larry Talbot.'

'Larry Talbot? I don't know a Larry Talbot.'

'He seems very pressing. Perhaps he's a hawker?'

Hanna Frankenstein asked him to take over the
responsibility for the porridge, and was on her way up
the stairs when Igor came hobbling in through the
kitchen door with an armful of wood. His eyes were
shining.

'Did I hear you say Larry Talbot?' he said.

'Yes,' said Aunt Frankenstein. 'Do you know him?'

'Do I know him? I certainly do,' said Igor. 'Only too
well.'

'Well, *who is he*?' Aunt Frankenstein almost exploded,
now thoroughly annoyed with all these refractory people
and monsters.

'You'll see, Aunt, you'll soon see,' tittered Igor. 'Oh,
so Larry Talbot's back again, is he? Now it's really getting like the old days.'

If looks could annihilate a person, Igor would not have
existed in that kitchen any longer. Hanna Frankenstein
strode up the stairs and into the entrance hall.

She and Frans had tried to clear up some of the worst
mess. The cobweb draperies had gone, as well as the rusty
armour, and the remains of a wood fire was smoking in

the fireplace. They had miraculously succeeded in providing a reasonably welcoming atmosphere, even if it were still somewhat gloomy. They had also hacked a pathway through the briars up to the front door, so that visitors could get in that way.

A middle-aged man with a puffy face was standing waiting in the hall. He didn't look exactly shabby, but his tweed jacket and trousers were unpressed and baggy, and he had great bags under his eyes, giving him the appearance of a man who had suffered greatly.

'Mr Talbot,' said Aunt Frankenstein, stepping forward. 'I am Hanna Frankenstein, Henry's aunt. In what way can I be of service?'

Talbot's forehead wrinkled into unhappy A-shaped lines, like a sorrowful dog as he licked his thick lips.

'Mrs Frankenstein, I've come on a very er ... painful errand. The whole matter is extremely difficult and painful to mention.' His small eyes were red-rimmed and exhausted as they flickered beneath his bushy eyebrows, accentuating the bags below.

'I can see that,' said Aunt Frankenstein discreetly. 'You look as if you needed a pick-me-up.'

She had heard Igor padding behind her on the stairs to eavesdrop, and she said sharply over her shoulder: 'Igor! Please go and get a large glass of sherry for Mr Talbot.'

'No, no,' said Talbot, taking a step forward in his unpressed trousers. 'You misunderstand me. Drink is not my problem.'

He paused and lowered his voice, his eyes sliding sideways.

'It's the moon,' he said.

'The moon?' said Aunt Frankenstein blankly.

'Yes, the moon, to put it baldly.' The lines on his forehead deepened and he looked very unhappy.

'In other words, you mean your hair's falling out? In that case, I think you should consult the local hairdresser.'

'No, no,' said Talbot. 'I mean the full moon.' He glanced sideways and took another step forward. 'My hair isn't falling out. On the contrary. Mrs Frankenstein, I'm a condemned man. I was bitten by a werewolf in my childhood.'

'Ow!' said Aunt Frankenstein.

'Yes, that's what I said when it happened.'

'Where did it bite you?'

'Here, on my arm.' Talbot pointed to his tweed jacket.

'No, I mean, where were you at the time?'

'Not far from here. And now I'm the scourge of the locality.'

The lines in Talbot's forehead deepened even further, like ravines, and again he licked his dry lips.

'Mrs Frankenstein. Tonight the moon is full again, and then I will be transformed into a werewolf again. I can already feel the early symptoms.'

A sound like a slight growl came out of his throat and he cleared his throat with embarrassment to stop himself.

Aunt Frankenstein had involuntarily taken a step backwards, but she persuaded herself that all this was naturally absolute nonsense, a case for a psychoanalyst, she was quite convinced. She retained her icy calm.

'Oh, yes? Or to be more precise, what do you want me to do about it?'

'Lock me up!' said Talbot. 'Your nephew often did me that service. Then he went away and, ever since then, I've been wandering round like an outlaw with no fixed base at all. I beg of you, lock me up in the east tower-room. Lock me in and, whatever happens, don't open the door.'

'That seems to me to be a fairly reasonable request,' said Aunt Frankenstein. She called over her shoulder, as she knew Igor was standing eavesdropping behind the door: 'Igor! Mr Talbot is stopping the night with us. Get the west tower-room ready.'

Igor came out into the hall, bowing humbly.

'Certainly, Missis.'

'No, not the west tower-room, if you don't mind,' said Talbot. 'The east tower-room.'

'Yes,' said Igor. 'Because Mr Frans is in the west tower-room.'

'Of course, yes,' said Hanna Frankenstein. 'I keep muddling the points of the compass.'

'And the full moon rises in the east,' said Talbot. 'That is of great significance to me. I only want to be prepared when it comes.'

'I see,' said Aunt Frankenstein, who was beginning to be thoroughly fed up with all this. 'Go on, now, Igor, and make up the bed in the wolf-lair. The east wolf-lair. Well, you'll have to excuse me, Mr Talbot, but I find it a trifle difficult to take all this seriously.'

'Mrs Frankenstein, I assure you,' said Talbot. 'It is all deadly serious. It could be quite literally, if you forget and open up the door. I become a wolf when the moon rises.'

A faint growl came out of him and again he cleared his throat uneasily.

Hanna Frankenstein walked towards the kitchen stairs.

'Mr Talbot,' she said. 'We've spoken about this enough now. If you wish to, you may become a whole zoo. I will *not* be opening the door. Good-day.'

A Nocturnal Hobby

'What did he want?' said Frans.

'Oh, nothing special. He only wanted to spend the night here.'

'I thought he looked a bit down.'

Frans raised the porridge spoon and dropped it demonstratively on to the empty plate. Monster was smiling broadly.

'Oh, look! He's eaten everything up!' said Aunt Frankenstein.

'I told him a story,' said Frans. 'The one about Hansel and Gretel. He liked it.'

He pushed up his glasses and got up from the table.

'Well, I think I'll go up to my room for a while. I must put my telescope together. I thought I would do a bit of moon-studying. There's a full moon tonight.'

'Thanks very much, I know that,' said Aunt Frankenstein. She had been just about to reveal something about Talbot, but then she hurriedly changed the subject to what Frans had brought up. 'I'd no idea you were an amateur astronomer. Fancy you keeping that a secret from me.'

'It's because it's a nocturnal hobby,' said Frans. 'We astronomers are a light-shy lot.'

'I thought that long case of yours contained golf-clubs,' said Aunt Frankenstein.

'No, that's my telescope,' said Frans. 'I'll go and set it up now. See you at dinner.'

He went upstairs.

'Well, his relationship to the moon seems rather more sensible than certain other people's,' muttered Aunt Frankenstein, turning to Monster. 'Time for your after-dinner rest now,' she said. 'Come on, no protests!'

She took the reluctant colossus by the hand and led him away.

The April evening was calm, the sky grey and red, a slight smell of smoke in the air. Aunt Frankenstein and Igor were clearing the briars outside the castle. Monster was still asleep and Frans was in his room.

Aunt Frankenstein paused and straightened up. She was beginning to get blisters on her hands. A blackbird was singing nearby.

'It really is the limit,' she said. 'Here we've got a newly resuscitated monster in the house and we can't even use him as a gardener.'

'He'll improve,' said Igor. 'He'll probably improve.'

He sniffed the air.

'I think they're burning leaves down in the village.'

'Yes, we ought to light a bonfire, too,' said Hanna Frankenstein. 'All these dry old bushes. But then Monster would go crazy, I suppose.'

'Yes, he can't stand fire,' said Igor. 'I remember in the old days, when the villagers came marching up with their torches. Heavens, you should have seen him then. He went quite crazy.'

'I remember Henry wrote in his letters that they were always running around with torches. There never seemed to be any peace. Not that I wish to defend Henry but, as far as I can make out, poor old Monster never got a chance to show what he could do. As soon as he went out for a whiff of fresh air, he got a torch thrust under his nose and a dog set on him. Is that so?'

'Yes, roughly,' said Igor. 'Roughly.' He blinked his red-rimmed eyes under his fringe, as he stood there with the shears in his hand.

Aunt Frankenstein lit a cigar. Her consumption of Brazilian cigars had gone down considerably since Monster had appeared.

'I think Henry is a good-for-nothing,' she said, blowing out a cloud of smoke. 'There's no doubt about it. But even if people happen to be good-for-nothings, or monsters, they must be given a chance. Don't you think? That's right, isn't it?'

'Yes, of course, of course,' said Igor.

'Because if all dogs were judged by their coats, I wonder how many would be allowed out. Talking of that . . . did you lock that Talbot creature up?'

'Yes, yes,' said Igor. 'Double-locked.'

'Funny creature. Don't you think?'

Igor tittered.

'Yes, he's a bit original, you could say.'

'What did you do with the key?'

'I left it in the door. Do you want me to go and get it?'

'No, no, spare your old legs,' said Aunt Frankenstein. 'It can stay there. No one will want to go up there, and that part of the castle isn't used. I think we'll call it a day now, Igor. I feel like taking a little walk. But if you'd go in and see to Monster for a while and make sure he doesn't get up to any mischief. He may have woken up now.'

'Certainly, Missis,' said Igor.

He limped away through the undergrowth, then suddenly stopped and peered down at the valley.

On the other side of the green valley, the village looked like a huddle of roofs, smoke rising here and there, a white strand of mist hovering above the roofs. A dog was barking in the distance. The evening was greyish-red and half-cloudy.

'What is it?' said Aunt Frankenstein. 'What are you staring at?'

'I thought I saw fire down there.'

'Did you? You said just now they were burning leaves down in the village, didn't you?'

'Yes, yes, of course . . .' said Igor, looking quickly up, then swiftly setting off like a scuttling rat. 'Have a nice walk, Missis!' he called back over his shoulder.

'What a funny way of behaving,' thought Aunt Frankenstein. But Igor was, as he himself had said about Talbot, a trifle original, and she didn't give the matter another thought. She was feeling it was high time for a glass of sherry, but she decided to take a walk first. It was a lovely April evening. She loved these misty spring evenings with their slightly spicy scent of smoking leaves in the distance, the blackbird's song clearer than ever. She saw a fat coal-black male perched on a twig in the undergrowth playing on his golden flute.

She walked past the great front entrance and noticed it was still far from high-class, the door rotten and overgrown with moss. That would have to be replaced, but there was plenty of time and she wasn't expecting any visitors. Talbot was only a chance caller. She wondered how he was getting on up there in the tower-room with his werewolf phobias. Poor thing, she thought, remembering his harrowed puffy face. So the man really believed he would turn into a werewolf. She could imagine him sitting up there in the ruined tower-room in a rat-chewed armchair, gazing at the sky in the east.

She couldn't see the moon yet, but most of the sky in the east was hidden by the massive stone walls of the castle.

The blackbird was singing at full throat behind her, no doubt already filled with the joys of spring.

She could hear hounds barking in the distance, almost like a whole pack. Who would be out hunting on a spring evening? Was that permitted at this time of year?

She turned the corner of the east wing of the castle ... and almost bumped into Frans.

'Ooops! You're out for a walk too, are you?' she said.

'Yes, I thought I'd get my circulation going before the night's observations,' said Frans. 'You get so cold behind a telescope at an open window.'

'I'm sure you do,' said Aunt Frankenstein. 'But if it gets too cold out there on the Milky Way, you'll have to come and have a glass of sherry with me.'

'Thanks very much,' said Frans, glancing up at the eastern sky. 'But I must hurry now, if you don't mind. The moon will soon be up.'

'Of course, please don't let me keep you,' said Aunt Frankenstein.

They parted and Hanna Frankenstein continued on her walk.

'Aunt Frankenstein,' Frans called after her. 'I hope you don't mind, but I'm going to shift my things over to the east tower-room ... you can see the moon better from there.'

'You do that,' she answered absent-mindedly, and they waved goodbye to each other.

She walked round the thick stone tower of the laboratory and continued along the north wall of the castle.

To think that she had never known about this nocturnal hobby of his! There was a lot you never knew about people, when it came to the point. But Frans was in many ways a man of surprises.

She stopped on the muddy path and looked down over the valley. The mountain fell steeply downhill only a few metres away from her feet. It was growing dark, mist and smoke hanging like a veil down there in the valley and, on the other side, the forest climbed up northern slopes, blueish-green in colour. She could see the village far away to the west, a huddle of misty roofs and smoking chimneys. She could make out the road that led up to the castle, by the twists and turns that appeared now and again between the clumps of trees in the valley. She remembered her own journey in the executioner's cart. But what was that red light glimmering down there? A heap of burning leaves? But it seemed to be moving. There was another light there.

She heard dogs barking again, clearer now, and echoing, as if the pack were up in the mountains.

She looked at the pocket-watch she had hanging on a chain round her neck. Half-past seven. High time for sherry.

She turned round and looked towards the east, where the moon was rising out of the mist, large, round and dark yellow.

She thought it funny about those two moon-watchers: Frans in one tower staring at the moon through a telescope, and Talbot in the other, gazing at the same planet, thinking he was going to turn into a wolf. Science in one room and superstition in the other.

Suddenly she realised what Frans had actually said . . . *that he was going to shift his things over to the east tower-room*! And she saw before her Talbot's haggard face as he had said: 'Lock me up and, whatever you do, don't open the door.'

At that moment, she heard a long drawn-out howl that made the blood in her veins turn cold. It was exactly like a wolf howling at the moon.

She hoped with all her heart that it wasn't Talbot starting up *his* nocturnal hobby.

The Werewolf

She heard the howling again, long drawn-out and plaintive as it echoed round the mountains in a hollow ghost-like manner, then blended with the baying of dogs that had now come even closer. Perhaps it had been a dog howling after all?

But in that case, who had let the dog in in the first place, because she could now hear quite clearly that the howling was coming from ... *up in the east tower-room*!

For a moment Hanna Frankenstein's blood turned as cold as mineral water in her veins.

Then she persuaded herself that this was all absolute nonsense and strode along the path above the precipice.

When she came round the moss-covered toolshed leaning drunkenly against the west wall of the castle, she at once saw the torches. Through the briars she and Igor had recently tamed, she saw a wavering mass of flames marching up towards the castle and again she heard the baying of hounds.

So the hunt was coming in this direction!

She could feel her nose turning ice-cold with fury.

So those ruffians weren't going to give her a chance, either.

Well, she would show them.

Swiftly, she ran over to the kitchen entrance and shouted for Igor, who came hobbling out into the murk with a lighted paraffin lamp in his hand.

'Yes?' he said, sounding frightened.

'Is Monster asleep?'

'He's just woken up.'

'Whatever happens, see he stays indoors. On no account must he be let out of the castle. The torches are on the march again.'

'I saw them, Missis,' said Igor, in a worried voice.

Aunt Frankenstein slammed the kitchen door shut, gave a twitch to her bun to make sure it was in reasonable order and then, upright and dignified, she walked to the front entrance, looking very smart in her black costume.

She stood waiting in the front doorway, her feet astride and arms crossed. She was icy calm now, knowing perfectly well what rôle she was going to play. The audience could come.

The first of them were coming up the slope, a group of dogs ahead, two alsatians, two hounds and an old bull-dog, all on leads, and while the alsatians were eagerly dragging their owners along by their leads, the bulldog looked like an ancient piece of furniture longing to be put in a museum. Just behind the dogs came a man she at once recognised . . . the guard. His face was red and shiny from all the strain and excitement, his yellow moustache hanging down like a dead leaf beneath his nose and his Tyrolean hat askew. He seemed rather askew himself, too, and was taking bandy-legged sidesteps in his hunts-man's green plus-fours. Behind him came a wall of large men she did not recognise, all of them holding burning torches in their hands, their faces red and glowing in the light of the flames. The massed standards of torches swayed and fluttered down on the hillside as far as the eye could see, snaking their way right down the road, and now she realised what the fire was she had seen down there in the valley.

The procession came to the front of the castle and

stopped, the dogs snapping and snarling, the torch-bearers muttering excitedly, their light falling on the weed-filled gravel patch in front of the entrance and Hanna Frankenstein's boots. The guard again noticed his own shoes were five sizes smaller, and that annoyed him very much indeed. He hooked his thumbs into his trouser-belt and said in a shrill voice:

'You no doubt know why we've come?'

'No, I certainly do not!' said Hanna Frankenstein. 'So we meet again so soon, do we? I had expectations for my journey home.'

'The pleasure is all yours,' said the guard rudely.

'Come to the point,' said Hanna Frankenstein. 'What do you want?'

She took out a cigar and asked the nearest torch-bearer for a light, but he seemed insulted by her boldness. In the crowd behind the guard, she recognised the station-master and the village innkeeper. The excited muttering grumbled on down the hill, the torches flaring against the night sky.

The guard fixed her with his swimming eyes beneath his Tyrolean hat; he was apparently more than half-seas over.

'You've woken up the Monschter!' he said indistinctly, pointing at her. 'Can you deny it?'

'No, I can't,' said Hanna Frankenstein. 'But I have to inform you that that was not my original intention.'

She heard a raucous laugh from down the hill and someone shouted: 'Tell that to the Marines!'

'As I said,' said Hanna Frankenstein, raising her voice. 'That was not my original intention. It was not until I saw what a state the castle was in that I realised I had to have the help of a pair of supernaturally strong arms. But I assure you ...'

She was interrupted again by a man shouting: 'The value of our houses goes down when we have to live near a monster!'

Another shouted: 'Go home! And take the Monster with you.'

The muttering rose to deafening proportions and Aunt Frankenstein had to shout to be heard.

'Gentlemen! I assure you Monster will not be allowed to leave the grounds this time. You can sleep safely down there in the village. Monster is going to help me restore the castle, that's all.'

But it was like talking to a burning wall.

'The Monster must go!' shouted a deep bass voice. That was the fair-haired blacksmith who was standing some way down the hill, his torch looking like an outsize match in his hand.

'Gentlemen!' Aunt Frankenstein said again. 'Listen to what I have to say! Listen *carefully* to what I have to say. Don't think for one moment I'm defending my nephew. No, Henry is a good-for-nothing and I agree. But I've come here to put things right again. *That's* why I'm here ... to clear the family name.'

'There's not enough soap and water in the whole of Bavaria to do that,' said the guard, his eyes sparkling when he heard the laughter he had caused. He looked round with satisfaction, his thumbs hooked in his braces now. Aunt Frankenstein felt like pulling his Tyrolean hat down over his ears, but she controlled herself, as that would hardly have helped her cause.

She glared at the nearest men, looking sharply from one to the next, avoiding looking at the guard so as not to get too angry.

'Are you all without faults yourselves?' she barked. 'Are you all as pure as driven snow? Have you never tried

avoiding paying taxes? Have you never driven when
you've had one too many? Or even done a bit of home-
brewing?'

The guard stiffened. He had a small still at home down
in his cellar. Did she know anything? No, that wasn't
possible, but he'd better go into the attack at once. He
raised his forefinger in the air and shouted:

'The Monster must go!'

'Yes!' they all yelled. 'The Monster must go!'

'Remember,' said the guard grandly, hooking his
thumbs into his braces again. 'This is an area with tra-
ditions of *culture*. In that castle . . .' he pointed. 'In that
castle Lord Byman and the great poet Jelly once stayed
the night . . .'

'For God's sake, Fritz,' hissed the innkeeper behind
him. 'Lord Byron and Shelley, they're called.'

'Well, anyhow, they stayed the night there once on
their way to Switzerland,' said the guard sullenly.

'As if I didn't know that!' said Hanna Frankenstein
emphatically. 'The Frankenstein family is related to
Shelley's wife.'

The innkeeper thrust his shiny face forward, his moustache long and black in the torchlight.

'But then you Frankensteins started getting up to all
this mischief and that was the end of poetry. That's when
philistinism came to the village.'

'Exactly!' said the guard. 'That's when philistinism
came to the village. When you came!'

Aunt Frankenstein felt as if she had been struck on the
head by lightning. That nasty little bully saying that . . .
and he presumably couldn't even spell the word *culture*!
The next moment, scarcely knowing where the words
came from she heard herself saying:

'NOW LISTEN TO ME! Before the end of the

summer, I will invite you all to a soirée here at the castle ... and then I'm damned if you won't hear Monster reciting poems by Shelley.'

In reply came a great deal of crude laughter and scornful remarks from down on the slope. But the men standing nearest to her were staring beyond her. When she turned round, she saw Frans running towards her in the gathering dark, his shirt torn and his hair standing on end. She had completely forgotten about him.

'Aunt! Aunt!' he yelled. 'He's got out!'

'But I told Igor to lock him in,' said Aunt Frankenstein almost desperately.

'Not Mon ... Monster,' stammered Frans. 'It's Talbot who's got out.'

At that moment they heard the sound of windows shattering in the castle and broken glass showered down into the undergrowth. Then a dark figure landed on all fours with a heavy rustling in the undergrowth, then rose and came towards them, crouching and walking with long jerky gliding strides. The flickering torchlight fell on him, and Hanna Frankenstein saw that he was unusually hairy. He was wearing nothing but a pair of trousers, his eyes glinting in the torchlight, not human eyes, nor were his nose and mouth especially human either – glittering white fangs protruding from the most prominent lower jaw she had seen for a long time ...

A great wave of terror ran through the so recently aggressive crowd, and shrill voices cried everywhere: 'The werewolf! It's the werewolf! Run for your lives!'

The crowd had already dispersed in wild flight down the hill.

What's Flapping in the Library?

'Don't you go baring your teeth at me,' said Hanna Frankenstein. 'I can bite, too, if needs be.'

So that was what a werewolf looked like, was it? She thought he looked like a cross between an alsatian dog and a gorilla in trousers. She could see no resemblance to Talbot, except perhaps the bags under his eyes, but they were hairy now, like a wolf's, an indefinite greyish-yellow colour.

'All werewolves are grey in the dark,' she thought.

The werewolf growled and leapt at her, but she side-stepped quickly and, unable to stop itself, the beast flew quite a way down the slope. She noticed he had no tail. The hillside was thick with fleeing people, their torches lying burning on the ground, and in the light of one of them she saw the guard's Tyrolean hat.

Frans appeared at her side again.

'Aunt! Hurry up indoors. He's dangerous!'

'I can't take the responsibility of that hairy thing running around all night. If anything happens, the villagers will blame us.'

She wondered how she could lure the werewolf in without being attacked herself.

The werewolf had stopped down the hill, apparently frightened by the many burning torches lying on the road. He snapped and snarled, running back and

forth with long gliding strides, now and again glancing hungrily up at Aunt Frankenstein and Frans, his
yellow eyes glittering in the firelight, his teeth gleaming
white.

Aunt Frankenstein tried calling to him as she would to
a dog.

'Come on then, come to Auntie. There's a good
werewolf.'

'Open the toolshed door,' she hissed to Frans over her
shoulder.

Slowly she began to retreat up towards the castle.

The werewolf came, crouching, his hairy fists clenched
at his chest as he bounded towards her with long loping
strides. Aunt Frankenstein recognised Talbot's baggy
trousers. He had no shoes on and his feet were hairy paws
with long claws.

'There we are. Come on then! Come on!'

Hanna Frankenstein had always been good with dogs,
and she hoped that would stand her in good stead this
time as well. She continued retreating backwards along
the castle wall, and heard behind her a creaking as Frans
opened the toolshed door.

She stopped in front of the open door and hissed
over her shoulder: 'Be ready to slam it again when I tell
you.'

The werewolf came closer, his appearance not exactly
that of a man's best friend, nor even that of a watch-dog.
(Any property that happened to be guarded by this
creature would be condemned to lie empty and un-
inhabited, abandoned by its owners as well.)

There were thin streaks of mist in the undergrowth
and, as if wading through white smoke, those horrible
paws and Talbot's trousers came nearer and nearer, the
hairy body crouching ready to leap, a gurgling sound

coming from the black snout, the fangs in his lower jaw gleaming.

'There you are. Give Auntie your paw now.'

She was aware that she was stretching things a bit far.

The werewolf growled hideously, its yellow eyes narrowing. Eyes narrowing was a bad sign. Aunt Frankenstein knew that of old. 'No?' she said. 'Then you'll have to go in to your kennel here. In! *In*, I say!'

Hanna Frankenstein had stepped aside just in time. With one great roaring hairy leap, the werewolf flew past her and tumbled straight into the murky darkness of the toolshed.

'Shut it!' shrieked Aunt Frankenstein.

The wooden door slammed shut. Frans was looking as if he were about to faint.

The werewolf roared out his rage inside the shed, which rattled and shook and creaked as he ran round and round among the garden tools, and it sounded like a huge rake scrabbling on the door as he scratched at it with his claws. The planks bulged outwards under his assaults and Aunt Frankenstein prayed with all her might that the shed would hold, shouting through the cracks in the door: 'Mr Talbot! No more nonsense now, thank you! You can stay in there until you learn how to behave. Then you can come into the castle like a decent human being and have a glass of sherry. But not a drop of any kind as long as you persist with that lower jaw, do you understand?'

A blood-curdling wolf-howl came out of the shed in reply.

Aunt Frankenstein looked exhaustedly at Frans. She was just a trifle pale.

'Frans, my dear,' she said. 'Would you go ahead and get out the corkscrew. Today really has been rather a strain.'

.　　.　　.　　.　　.

Seven hours later, a small group of pale people was gathered round a bottle of dry sherry, a Manzanilla, in the castle library. The moon had gone down and it was growing light outside. Through the library window – a patchwork of cracked panes and pieces of cardboard – the grey light of dawn was filtering; falling over the round table with the sherry bottle and a three-branched candlestick containing the stumps of dripping candles, over the rat-chewed leather armchairs . . . Aunt Frankenstein, Frans and Larry Talbot. It also fell on to the book cases full of similarly rat-chewed and weather-beaten volumes, and on to the large sooty open fireplace, where the remains of a fire had begun to collapse into faintly tinkling embers and white ash. The morning would soon be there, and not one of the three had had a wink of sleep.

Aunt Frankenstein and Frans had sat there all night, taking it in turns to keep watch on the toolshed, and Larry Talbot had just come. Igor had let him out, after checking through a knot-hole that the attack was over. Talbot's puffy face was pale and harrowed, his clothes baggier than ever. But he had been up to the east tower-room to smarten himself up a bit for sherry, as it was his habit to wear only trousers when he was a werewolf.

'Tell me,' said Aunt Frankenstein. 'Are you often like this?'

Talbot looked up in torment from his sherry glass, his forehead deeply furrowed.

'No, only at full-moon. But nowadays it afflicts me on the following two nights as well.'

'I can't really understand the moon being to blame for all this,' said Frans. 'As an astronomer, I can't accept that.'

'But the fact remains,' said Talbot. 'I'd give anything to be rid of it.'

'Mr Talbot,' said Aunt Frankenstein, grasping the bottle. 'Some more sherry?'

'Thank you. It does me good. I always get such a terrible headache after these attacks.'

'Yes, you do look as if you had a really bad hangover,' said Aunt Frankenstein, suppressing a yawn and making as if to rise to her feet. 'Now, gentlemen, if you'll excuse me, I think I'll try and get myself a wink or two before sunrise.'

'Oh, don't say that,' said Frans. 'It makes me think of the legend of Dracula.'

'That's all we need now, that he should appear and want to stay the night,' said Aunt Frankenstein. 'My dear Frans, before we go, would you mind opening the window for a moment. It would be nice to get some fresh morning air.'

Frans rose, mumbling about the room in fact being very smoky, and he managed to open one of the two big windows without the remaining panes falling out of the frames. The window creaked and screeched as it slid up.

The damp morning air poured in, smelling of dew and wet earth. It was almost light out now. In the distance, a blackbird was singing and, somewhere closer, crows were squawking and spoiling the song. Frans thrust his head out of the window and looked towards the east. The sky above the mountains was turning pink.

Suddenly he jumped as something large and black came flapping through the air, straight at him! He swung away from the window and raised his arm to protect himself. Against the sky, he could see two wings like open umbrellas, and in between them a grinning cat-like head with slanting glittering eyes and sharp fangs. *It* flapped into the room, fluttering and rustling as Aunt Frankenstein shouted: 'Frans, get that crow out!'

76

'That's no crow!' said Frans, his hair on end. 'Don't you see what it is? It's a large bat. A vampire bat!'

The vampire flapped round the library once, dust and cobwebs falling from the bookcases in the draught from its wings. Aunt Frankenstein and Larry Talbot had leapt to their feet and were holding their hands in front of their faces. Once again it flapped round with rustling wings... then it stalled in the air and stayed hovering above the floor. Out of the wings, like black draperies, fell ... a figure! There was a rustle of cloth and a pair of patent-leather shoes were heard landing on the parquet floor.

And there he stood, elegantly clad in tail-coat and cape, pale as death and with a smile on his black lips ... Count Dracula!

Can a Werewolf be Cured?

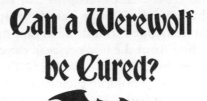

A great draught whistled through the library and there was a smell of cold stone, as in an old church. Talbot's lined face lit up.

'Why, hullo, Dracula! So you're out flying at this time of day, are you?'

'Talbot?' said Dracula. 'Are you here too?'

It was a reunion between two condemned men whose ways had crossed several times in this part of the world.

Dracula spoke in a veiled slightly nasal tone of voice, and his appearance was extremely elegant and aristocratic. He turned to Aunt Frankenstein and Frans with a stiff bow.

'Madame! Sir!' he said. 'Allow me to introduce myself. I am Count Dracula. I was just passing and I saw a light on in the library. It is good to see new blood has come to the house.'

His thin black lips curled into an enigmatic smile.

'Well, Count Dracula,' said Hanna Frankenstein. 'That was a nice little transformation scene. Shaking yourself out of almost nothing. And what can we do for you?'

'To be honest, and to use a metaphor, I have been out all night flitting like a bee from flower to flower. Now I long to come to rest.'

'In other words,' said Hanna Frankenstein. 'You want to get down into the coffin and close the lid over yourself?'

Dracula swept his black cape with its blood-red lining closer round him, bowing weakly:

'I hear, Madame, that you are well acquainted with my unfortunate fate.'

A tomb-like chill came from his figure, his eyes burning with a cold black glow in his white face.

'Well,' said Aunt Frankenstein. 'I know the main features of it. You're a typical nocturnal creature, you can't stand sunlight, and you occasionally transform yourself into a bat.'

'*I* prefer to say vampire.'

Dracula smiled again, his white fangs gleaming inside the black lips. He gave a slightly hunted glance out of the window, where they could see from the sky that the sun was rising. He bowed once again and his smooth black hair shone like the polished marble on a sarcophagus.

'Madame, if you will excuse me, time is getting on. In his day, young Mr Henry used to have a coffin always ready for me down in the cellar. Would you permit me to leave you now and go to rest?'

'Certainly, certainly,' said Hanna Frankenstein. 'Rest in peace.'

'Unfortunately, that is just what I do not do,' said Dracula in sepulchral tones. 'I am condemned to eternal unrest. *Au revoir*, then.'

He flung out his cape like a pair of wings, beginning to shrink and turn into a vampire before their very eyes. With a hissing sound, his body was sucked up from the floor in a drapery-like movement and became the flapping black figure of a large bat.

'I suppose he'll go as the crow flies to the cellar. That's

quicker of course. But I thought he was nicer as a human being. Talbot, would you mind opening the door for him?'

The vampire flapped once round the walls before vanishing through the door. There was a smell of dust and cold stone, a tomb-like chill in the draught from those terrible rustling wings.

Talbot closed the door.

'We condemned men, things aren't easy for us,' he said, his forehead deeply furrowed.

'Yes, I can see it's hard work,' said Hanna Frankenstein. 'Especially with all those quick changes of rôle. You're nicer as a human being, too, for that matter. Those fangs you acquired last night, they're not at all becoming.' She suppressed another yawn. 'Yes, now I'm going to do as Dracula has, go off to bed before the sun rises.'

'That'll be any minute now,' said Frans, over by the window, looking out. He was slightly pale. This accumulation of bizarre figures was beginning to get on his nerves.

Aunt Frankenstein was standing with her hand on the doorhandle, on her way out.

'I forgot to ask the bat what he wanted for breakfast. What does a thing like that eat? Birdseed or cheese . . . or both?'

'Aunt,' said Frans gravely, pushing up his glasses. 'I don't think you've really taken it in. Dracula is a vampire. He is a ghost who sucks blood from living people.'

Hanna Frankenstein suppressed yet another yawn. She was very tired.

'Blood? Oh, yes. I'll tell Igor before I go to bed. One tea, two coffees and one blood. Goodnight, boys.'

She left.

Frans stared at the closed door.

'She's tired, of course, but I don't think she really took me seriously.'

'She didn't take me seriously at first, either,' said Talbot.

They heard a cock crow in the distance through the open window, and others echoing in reply from various directions. The morning mist lay white in the valley, and over the forest-covered mountains in the north, they could see an orange-coloured light.

'The sun's rising now,' said Talbot. 'I hope Dracula had time to turn in.'

'Yes, Talbot,' said Frans. 'Before we do the same, I must get it clear about your peculiar sickness. I don't doubt what you say, because I have a few little scratches from our meeting last night.'

'I'm truly sorry,' said Talbot. 'If only Igor had taken out the key.'

'It wasn't your fault. But Talbot . . .' Frans pushed his glasses up again. 'It's the part the moon plays in it all that I can't understand. There isn't in the whole of astronomy a case of such a peculiar cosmic influence.'

He paused and looked searchingly at Talbot, who was now striding up and down the creaking weather-beaten parquet floor.

'Don't be offended . . . but I wondered whether it could be due to you yourself *believing* so strongly that you will turn into a werewolf.'

'I don't know about believing,' said Talbot huffily. 'I just *do* become one.'

'Yes, but the power of belief is very great. I wonder what would happen if you tried applying a slightly more scientific attitude to the whole problem. What do you say, Talbot . . . let's meet by the telescope this evening, and try to take it from a more astronomical viewpoint when it starts again?'

Talbot stopped striding and looked very interested.

'I'm prepared to try anything. That's truly noble of you, Frans.'

'Oh, please don't mention it,' said Frans. 'I've always dreamt of being able to do something slightly beyond the everyday run of things.'

'But I must warn you,' said Talbot. 'You're taking a terrible risk.'

The Moon Rises Again

'Good evening, Aunt! Here I am with your coffee.'

Igor put the tray down on a tatty chair and drew back the curtains in Hanna Frankenstein's bedroom.

Hanna Frankenstein raised one eyelid beneath her night-cap.

'Uh? What? What's the time?'

'Nearly seven,' said Igor. 'In the evening.'

Hanna Frankenstein propped herself up on her elbow.

'Heavens, then I've slept all day! Where are the others?'

'Mr Talbot and Mr Frans have just gone up to the east tower-room to make astronomical observations. Monster is planting violas and pansies round the front door, and the Count has not yet got up.'

'So he got to the coffin before sunrise, then,' said Aunt Frankenstein.

She waved Igor's offer of sugar away.

'No, thanks. No sugar.'

Igor took a sugar-lump, heaved himself up on to a chair and dangled his legs.

'Yes, but only just in the nick of time, as they say. If you remember, we put all the dirty washing in that old coffin the other day.'

He peered at her.

Hanna Frankenstein sat up in bed.

'Good gracious, yes! I'd quite forgotten. What did Dracula say?'

Igor tittered.

'He was not at all pleased to find pants and towels in his night-lair ... I mean his day-lair. He said he had never experienced anything like it in all his life as a vampire.'

'Oh, well,' said Aunt Frankenstein, dipping a rusk in her coffee. 'He can't think he's above the trivialities of everyday life just because he flaps around in that grand manner at night. If the shoes don't fit, he'll just have to go elsewhere for his accommodation. And Monster, then? How's he?'

'Bad, Aunt, bad,' said Igor, sliding down from the chair and limping over to one of the windows. 'Look for yourself.'

Aunt Frankenstein's bedroom was on the ground floor and faced two points of the compass, partly to the east and partly towards the front of the castle. She stretched out her hand for her dressing-gown and padded across to the south window, where Igor was holding the curtain back. In the pinkish April dusk out there, she saw Monster sitting on the ground, his back against a great oak tree. He looked like a tired child, his huge legs stretched straight out in front of him and the ragged straw hat down over his nose. The impression of a large child was strengthened by the little trowel he had in his hand. An inquisitive bird was perched on one of his boots, its tail whipping up and down.

'Heavens above!' said Aunt Frankenstein. 'I wish those big mouths down in the village could see him now.'

She went back to the bed.

'Igor,' she said. 'We must have done something wrong when we woke him up. Do you think he got too little current through those gadgets in his neck?'

'Yes, I'm beginning to think the thunderstorm wasn't great enough,' said Igor. 'I'm really beginning to think that.'

Hanna Frankenstein sat down on the bed, looking both tired and troubled.

'Igor,' she said. 'I've done something foolish.'

'Have you? What have you done?'

Igor looked like a bright old hyena sniffing out something tasty.

'Last night I promised the villagers that before the summer was over they would be able to hear Monster reciting poetry by Shelley.'

'Oh, that's quite something, that is.'

Red spots appeared on Hanna Frankenstein's cheeks.

'When they accused the Frankenstein family of bringing philistinism to the locality. Did you ever hear such a thing!'

She got up again and had to walk off her fury on the cold floor. Igor gazed with fascination at her large flat feet and long knobbly toes.

'I thought I'd show them,' she went on, putting her hands on the tiled stove. 'But I think I've bitten off more than I can chew. That poor thing out there doesn't look as if he could even turn the pages of an anthology.'

Igor peered out through the south window.

'It's clouding over a little over there,' he said. 'Who knows, perhaps we'll have a chance to recharge him a little?'

'We can but hope,' said Hanna Frankenstein wearily, looking out through the other window and seeing the moon rising into the sky out of a cloud-bank, dark yellow like a ripe melon. It was not perfectly round, only almost full. Good, she thought at first, until she remembered Talbot's words, that he could be afflicted by his werewolf attacks on the two days following the full moon as well.

She turned to Igor.

'Where did you say Talbot was?' she said.

'Up in the east tower-room,' said Igor. 'With Mr Frans.'

A Scientific Experiment

The long brass telescope was mounted on its three legs, pointing through the open tower window in the direction of the moon. Larry Talbot was sitting in a shabby armchair oozing stuffing, his eye glued to the eyepiece. Frans was standing beside him with a chart of the moon in his hand.

'Talbot,' he said nervously, 'don't let the telescope go now. And try to breathe slowly.'

The evening wind was chilly and the moon-chart rustled in the draught. Despite the cold, sweat was pouring off Talbot's forehead.

'I must just take off my tie,' he said in a hoarse worried voice.

Frans glanced over his shoulder. His retreat was covered, the door to the tower-room ajar. He swallowed dryly and tried to make his voice as steady as possible.

'Talbot, now look quite calmly at the moon. The moon is a planet, a satellite of the earth. You must take this scientifically now. If you compare it with the moon-chart here, you'll see those dark patches on the surface of the moon called seas. There, for instance, is the Sea of Serenity...' He pointed to the chart... 'And just beside it is the Sea of Tranquillity, or Mare Tranquillitatis, as it's called in Latin ...'

Talbot cleared his throat, as a growl kept trying to get out of his throat. Frans heard it and discreetly shifted one foot nearer to the exit.

'The Sea of Tranquillity, Talbot,' he said encouragingly, in the belief that the words themselves might have a calming effect. 'Say it after me, now, Talbot. The Sea of Serenity ... the Sea of Tranquillity ...'

Talbot repeated hoarsely: 'The Sea of Clarity ... the Sea of the Tranquillity ... Marrrrrre Trrrrranquillitatis!'

His voice grew more and more inhuman and he could not keep back the growls.

'And look there, that's the Sea of Danger,' he said with a sudden wildness in his voice. 'Sea of Dangerrrrrrrrrrr!' It was no longer a human-being speaking.

Frans had hitherto been mostly looking at the moon and the moon-chart. When he shifted his gaze to the telescope, he saw round the brass tube a pair of hands that had not been there a moment ago, their contours a trifle blurred, apparently growing and changing shape, the nails growing longer and more crooked, and grey hairs beginning to grow on the backs of the hands ...

'Talbot!' he said sternly. 'Pull yourself together, Talbot! It's only superstition! The moon is a planet with a density of 0.61 ...'

But Talbot's face showed him that Talbot was no longer susceptible to scientific experiments. His face was blurred, changing shape, his mouth and eyes twitching, his beard beginning to grow, grey hairs appearing everywhere ... on his forehead and cheeks, his nose lengthening and turning black at the end, his lower jaw protruding ... and out of the dribbling lower lip came the predatory teeth like terrifying white skittles.

Frans was already on his way out of the door.

When he had slammed it shut and locked it behind him, he heard the werewolf hurling himself at the door with a primaeval snarl. He had escaped at the very last moment.

He turned round, his knees shaking, and thumped angrily on the door.

'Talbot!' he shouted. 'Can't you hear what I say! That's all nothing but superstition!'

Mrs Frankenstein, You are an Unusually Full-blooded Lady...

It was somewhat later on in the evening. The black clouds on the horizon had come closer and thunder was rumbling in the distance. Aunt Frankenstein was in the library reading an old book about vampires she had found on the shelves. She was smoking a cigar, sipping sherry and leaning over the book to be able to read in the light from the flickering candles. The lighting problem was one of the things that would have to be put right soon, she reckoned.

The dark windows were lit up by a blue flash of lightning, but a long time went by before the thunder came, a dull rumble rolling away in the distance. It began to rain, large drops rattling on the windowpanes.

Aunt Frankenstein read that vampires originated in Transylvania, a wild mountainous tract in Romania. Vampirism ran in families in a complicated way, from family to family. A vampire lived a living death and never rested in peace in his grave, condemned for ever to go out at night in search of the blood of living people. And a vampire could only be killed by a stake being driven through his heart while he was asleep in his coffin in the daytime.

'Rather cowardly,' Aunt Frankenstein thought, 'attacking a sleeping person like that.' She had always had a strong sense of fair play.

The book also said that you could protect yourself from a vampire by rubbing garlic into doors and windows. She had taken her daily garlic tablet, which she always did during the dark winter months, so presumably she would not be in danger from the vampire.

She shut the book with a snort. 'Superstition and cops-and-robbers stuff!' she thought. Dracula was a skilful illusionist, that she was sure of, and he could certainly appear in a circus with his bat number. But ghost! Oh, no, they couldn't tell her stories about ghosts. There was a natural explanation for almost everything, and she still believed that Larry Talbot was a case for psycho-analysis. Dracula probably was, too. Aunt Frankenstein was pessimistic about many things and had a gloomy attitude to life, but she still believed in people's great variability . . . it was her great shining light in the Vale of Tears that stubbornly continued to call itself civilisation.

She put down her dead cigar stump and sipped at her sherry. There was a knock on the door.

'Come in!' she called.

The door opened with a slow creak and a black-clad figure in tails could just be seen in the darkness, the lining of his cape glowing red as blood.

'Good evening, Madame.' The voice was veiled and a trifle nasal.

'Well, look who's here!' said Hanna Frankenstein. 'Count Dracula. So you have got up?'

'I was woken by the noise on the floor above.'

Dracula came into the room, his patent-leather shoes tapping on the parquet floor.

'Oh, really?' said Aunt Frankenstein. 'Yes, that was Frans trying to cure Talbot's werewolf-fever with a dose of astronomy. But it didn't work very well.'

'And how did things go for Frans?'

Dracula was standing by her armchair and she could smell the breath of chill and cold stone on his cape.

'A slight scratch, that's all. But please, do sit down, Count Dracula.'

'Thank you, Madame, but I prefer to stand if you don't mind. For blood-circulation reasons, you understand.'

She reckoned he had given the word 'blood' an unnecessarily ambiguous emphasis. Thunder rumbled again in the distance, slightly nearer now, it seemed to her. Dracula was standing stiffly upright beside her armchair, his face white, his eyes glitteringly black in the light of the candles. 'A rather handsome man, really,' she thought. 'A trifle bloodless, perhaps.'

Bloodless! She shivered. Had he come to see her in his capacity as a hungry mosquito?

She got up and grasped the sherry bottle.

'Count Dracula, may I offer you a glass of sherry?'

Dracula took a step nearer, a deathly passion glinting in his black eyes. There was no doubt about it, the man was certainly handsome. Tall, too. Tall and handsome.

'Count Dracula, a glass of Manzanilla?'

'Madame,' he said in a subdued voice. 'All drinks lose their allure in comparison with you ...'

'Oh, please!' said Hanna Frankenstein. 'I suppose you say that to all old women. But I haven't much in the bank, I assure you.'

'Mrs Frankenstein!'

He was quite close to her now, his eyes glinting so it

seemed to her that she could see the mist-shrouded mountains of Transylvania in his pupils.

'They told me you were a lady of mature years. But in my opinion you are an unusually full-blooded lady ... it makes my head whirl to see the blood throbbing in your beautiful throat ...'

She reckoned he really was taking liberties now! If she had had her umbrella there, she would have hit him on the head with it.

'Now listen, Count Dracula!' she said sharply. 'Let's take things a little pianissimo, shall we?'

Dracula took a lightning step back, as if he had discovered a snake wound round her neck, his whole face expressing sudden horror.

'Oh, damnation!' he half hid his face behind his cape. 'You've been eating garlic.'

'I cannot deny that,' said Hanna Frankenstein. 'So what?'

'If there is anything vampires cannot stand,' said Dracula, indistinctly behind his cape. 'It's the smell of garlic.'

'What a pity,' said Hanna Frankenstein. 'I simply love garlic. I can eat any amount of it. It's been in my blood since my youth in Paris.'

'In your blood, too?' Dracula's eyes widened with horror, and he took yet another step towards the door.

'My dear Count Dracula,' said Aunt Frankenstein. 'You do look pale and drawn, I must say. I wonder whether it is some form of iron deficiency. Or is your diet a trifle one-sided? Have you never heard of a balanced diet?'

At that moment, someone knocked on the door, and Dracula jumped.

'Come in!' cried Hanna Frankenstein.

The door opened and Igor peered in.

'Oh, excuse me,' he said when he saw Dracula. 'I'm sorry if I'm disturbing you.'

'Did he have to sound so insinuating?' thought Hanna Frankenstein.

Dracula stepped forward.

'You're not disturbing me in the slightest, Igor,' he said. 'I was just on my way out. Headlong. Madame ... with your permission.'

With a swift drapery-like motion, he did his bat trick and flapped out through the door.

Lightning Strikes

'What was that, Igor?' said Aunt Frankenstein.

'It sounds as if the thunder's coming closer. I wondered whether we should get the laboratory ready to give Monster a bit of a recharge.'

'Perhaps it'd be worth a try. Where is he?'

'He's out there under the oak.'

'In this weather? That won't do him any good. We must tell him to come in.'

Aunt Frankenstein rushed out into the corridor, followed by Igor, and they both hurried to a disused room at the other end of the castle, opened the rotting window and looked out. Monster was sitting there as before, down under the old oak tree. They could just see him there in the dark, his long legs stretched out. It was pouring with rain that was rustling in the few dry leaves left at the top of the tree.

'Frankie!' called Aunt Frankenstein. 'Frankie, dear! Get up and come on in! You should never sit under a tree in a thunderstorm.'

She was just going to tell him the risk of being struck by lightning, but she never got that far.

The very next second, the rain-soaked darkness was split asunder by a violent flash of lightning like a thick tree-trunk of greenish-white light ... a direct contact between heaven and earth, and the clap of thunder was tremendous. Aunt Frankenstein and Igor were thrown back from the window by the pressure waves, both deafened and blinded.

When they again got up on to their trembling legs, they were both convinced Monster was by now beyond all possible help and a cautious glance out of the window confirmed their worst fears. The oak tree had split from top to bottom, the white surfaces glowing in the dark in the shape of a great gaping V. There was a smell of electricity and warm wood . . .

With a great effort, they managed to switch their gaze to the ground.

Monster was *standing* down there, upright and sturdily astride, his seven-league boots heavily anchored in the gravel, his shoulders revealing the great weight and strength of an ox, and he was just whipping off the silly straw hat and looking contemptuously at it. Then he flung it away with a scornful gesture and strode across to the front entrance of the castle, a greenish glow of surplus energy shimmering above his flat skull and all round his whole enormous body.

'Recharged!' said Igor. 'I've never seen him like that before.'

'To work!' shrieked Hanna Frankenstein. 'To work! Now at last there will be some kind of style about the House of Frankenstein.'

Two days later, at about the same time in the evening, a clean newly-mangled cloth was on the dining-table on the first floor. The stars were shining down through the skylights on to the supper plates and the four people sitting round the table. Candles were alight in two tall candelabras, a scene that would have gladdened the heart of the old baron and his highly original sense of cosiness. There was a smell of paint and wax-polish in the room, perhaps rather too strong for a sensitive nose and, in the background, they could hear a busy hammering, the whole castle ringing with powerful blows.

From her place at the end of the table, Hanna Frankenstein lifted up the serving-dish.

'Count Dracula, a little more black pudding?'

The Count looked hollow-eyed up from his plate.

'Thank you, Madame, but no more for me, thank you.'

'Are you sure? You should eat more, you know. I think you're looking unusually pale this evening.'

'Madame,' said Dracula. 'I have not had a wink of sleep owing to all that hammering.'

Frans looked up from his plate. He was also looking paler than usual.

'It's good that he's so industrious, but he hammers away all day and all night,' he said, pushing up his glasses, which immediately slid down again.

'Yes, that flash of lightning must have known what it was striking,' said Talbot.

He was looking considerably better than usual. His puffy face had more colour and the tortured lines on his forehead had gone.

'Well, gentlemen,' said Aunt Frankenstein. 'You must agree that it's pretty fantastic. In two days, he's repaired the whole of the dining-room, and now he's tackling the rest of the castle. That flash of lightning really did come as a gift from on high.'

Igor came in wearing an ill-fitting butler's jacket and went round with the serving dish.

'Mr Frans, may I offer you a little more black pudding?'

'No, no, no more, thank you very much all the same,' said Frans.

'Mr Talbot,' said Igor. 'Won't you just try a little, at any rate?'

'No, thank you,' said Talbot very firmly. 'No more blood for me, thank you, I hope.'

He had eaten nothing but a little green salad.

'So you really think you're cured now?' said Aunt Frankenstein.

'I hardly dare believe it myself,' said Talbot. 'But last night there was no transformation. That was the second attempt we made by the telescope. I suddenly felt nothing but a burning scientific interest in the moon and quite forgot about werewolf phobias. Thanks to Frans, here.'

They all looked at Frans, who blushed like a schoolboy.

'Oh, it was nothing,' he said, looking down at his plate.

'You see, Talbot,' said Hanna Frankenstein. 'I said it was all some kind of imagination. You'll see, Count Dracula, there'll be a cure for you, too.'

'Oh, Madame,' said Dracula. 'My case is quite hopeless.'

'I don't believe that for one moment,' said Aunt Frankenstein. 'I think every person who has no place in society feels like a wandering ghost, just like you. I think you ought to go back to Transylvania and look for an honest job. If you can find one.'

An expression of melancholy flitted across Dracula's pale face and he gazed hollow-eyed down at his plate, on which lay half a slice of black pudding.

'In spite of everything,' he said. 'The question is whether I wouldn't prefer to remain a vampire ... to adjusting to a life of these black slices.'

'Yes, Aunt,' said Frans. 'If you'll excuse me asking, but what is this extraordinary dish?'

'This?' said Aunt Frankenstein cheerfully. 'Black pudding is an old-fashioned dish made of blood I've had them make up for me at the butcher's down in the village. It was supposed to be a surprise for Count Dracula.'

'A very kind thought, Madame,' said Dracula.

'Igor,' he went on in sepulchral tones. 'Would you mind getting me some blackcurrant jelly.'

Hanna Frankenstein began to see the future with slightly rosier eyes. The flash of lightning had thrown a ray of hope on to what had been worrying her most recently, her hasty promise to the villagers of a poetry evening with recitals by Monster.

After supper, she went in search of the hammering giant, who was repairing the great banqueting hall at full speed by the light of two flaring torches. He had also shed his terror of fire and was at the top of a ladder, fitting new wood into the rotting roof-beams. The torches in the racks on the walls threw his gigantic shadow over the whole hall. Aunt Frankenstein stopped at the foot of the ladder, seeing in her mind's eye what the hall would look like in a few months' time, decorated for a banquet with candles and garlands, and filled with people on the benches along the walls. She saw Monster making his entrance, dressed-up and summer-fresh, perhaps with a rose in his buttonhole, a copy of the Collected Works of Shelley under his arm ...'

Well, perhaps she was rushing ahead too fast. In the light of the torches, she leafed through Shelley's Collected Works, waiting for a suitable moment to speak to Monster. He had not yet realised she was there, and she was afraid he would fall off the rickety ladder if she called up to him.

The hammering went on above her head, the torch-light flickering over the huge hall, and as she stood below the ladder, the fat book in her hand, it suddenly seemed to her that she was in an empty theatre and was rehearsing a part. Of course! The book was her script and the hammering was the work being carried out in the wings.

Before she herself knew how it happened, she was standing in the middle of the hall declaiming in a powerful voice from the epic drama *Prometheus Unbound* . . .

After a while, she became aware that the hammering had stopped.

She fell silent herself and turned round to find Monster standing behind her with a hammer in his hand, listening devoutly, his eyes shining behind half-closed eyelids, his hair hanging sweatily down over his forehead like wet grass over a precipice, a smile playing over his lips, the cathode and anode glinting in the torchlight. He raised his great hands in the shrunken jacket and made a gesture of appeal to her to go on.

'Oh, Frankie, my dear,' said Aunt Frankenstein in embarrassment. 'I didn't know I had an audience.'

All her worries seemed to have blown away at one go. She realised now that Monster liked poetry. She was sure she would now be able to fulfil her promise before the summer was over.

All she had to do was to set to work.

She held out the book.

An Invitation to the Full Moon

It was a boiling hot day in the middle of August. The guard and the station-master were ambling along the empty village street towards the inn, hardly able to lift their feet. They dragged their way past the inn's usual entrance and went on round to the tables outdoors at the back. In the patchy shade of the arbour, Irmgard was sitting embroidering a cloth, her face red and perspiring. She looked up when she heard their steps, blew the flies away from her face and tossed back her blonde plaits.

The guard and the station-master sank down on to chairs.

'So you're all alone, are you, Irmgard? No customers today?'

The guard put his peaked cap down on the table, revealing the deep red mark on his forehead.

'It's too hot, I expect,' said Irmgard. 'No one can be bothered to get here.'

'Incredible, isn't it?' said the station-master. 'I was just starting to boil, down at the station.'

'You should see what it's like on duty on the train,' said the guard. 'The track was buckled at Himmelsdorff and the last train had to be cancelled. Irmgard, my dear, a beer please, before I die.'

'And a sweet sherry for you, Helmut?' said Irmgard.

101

'No, no,' said the station-master. 'I'll have a beer, too, for once.'

The guard's eyes widened.

'What? Are you sick?'

'Yes,' said the station-master. 'Sick of the heat and all the chatter about my drinking habits.'

Irmgard called over her shoulder.

'Gretchen, my little one, two beers, please.'

'Two beers ... right!' came from inside the inn, and a few moments later out came a fair-haired girl with two frothing tankards in her hands. This was the couple's eight-year-old daughter, who helped them during the summer holidays. She was the image of her mother and had freckles on her cheeks like cinnamon on a bun.

'Have you heard the latest?' said Irmgard, leaning over her embroidery. 'They say the werewolf's cured.'

The guard wiped the froth off his moustache.

'What? Larry Talbot?'

'Yes. The butcher says so. He'd heard it from the post-lady. Talbot had been down to the post-office to send a telegram to his old mother in America to tell her he was better again. And the post-lady can confirm it's true. She'd met him herself the last time the moon was full, and she was terrified then, of course, as that was long before that telegram. But he's become clean-shaven and as nice as anything, and he just greeted her politely and said wasn't the moonlight beautiful.

'No, really?' said the station-master. 'Just fancy that.'

'Well, I won't believe that until I've seen it with my own eyes,' said the guard.

'And what's more, I'll have you know,' said Irmgard. 'The other day I was out picking raspberries in the mountains, and suddenly I heard someone calling: "*Oh woe! Alas! Oh, pain, pain ever, for ever!*" And who did I see

102

sitting there on a stone in the sun, declaiming poetry out of a book, if not the Monster!'

'But that's absolutely unbelievable,' said the station-master.

Then they heard steps on the gravel and a glistening perspiring corpulent figure appeared in the garden entrance, the innkeeper back from an errand to the butcher's. He had a piece of paper in his hand, a small poster with handwritten lettering on it.

'Now you men, and you Irmgard, just you listen to this,' he said breathlessly. 'And you, Gretchen; I didn't see you at first, my love. This poster is pinned up all over the village. Just you listen.'

He read out aloud from the poster.

To all cultured inhabitants of the village of Frankenstein and its surroundings. You are hereby invited to a little soirée at the newly restored castle on Friday 13th August at six o'clock.

Programme

1. *Our neighbour in space . . . popular science lecture on the moon by Lawrence Talbot.*
2. *Prometheus Unbound . . . a lyrical intermezzo with Frankenstein Junior.*

Welcome all!
Hanna Frankenstein

P.S. *Dogs and torches need not be brought.*

'There!' said the innkeeper. 'What do you say to that?'

'Well I'm blowed!' said the station-master.

'Friday the thirteenth of August,' said the guard, leafing suspiciously through his diary. 'Let's see . . . but the moon will be full then!' He looked at the others, his moustache drooping like dry grass. 'Never again will I go up there when the moon is full, never again in my whole life,' he went on. 'If you've ever been eye to eye with a werewolf, once is more than enough.'

'But he's cured now,' said Irmgard.

'Do you expect me to believe that?' said the guard. 'Don't you see, it's another trick the old woman's up to, to lead us all to destruction.'

'You can't be scared, Fritz?' said the station-master teasingly.

'Scared? Me? Didn't I go first, ahead of all of you, that time in April?'

'But you needn't go first this time,' said the station-master. 'I can do that, if needs be.'

Gretchen thrust her freckled cinnamon-bun face forward:

'Can I come with you on Friday, Mother, and see the werewolf and the Monster? Uncle Fritz can stay and look after the inn for us and then the whole family could go.'

'That's a good idea, my girl,' said the innkeeper. 'What do you say to that, Fritz?'

The guard went scarlet with anger.

'Of course I'm coming too!' he said. 'You must see that. If I'm not on duty, that is.'

The Procession of Guests

But the guard was not on duty on the Friday. He and the station-master and the innkeeper's family all trooped up towards the castle together on the warm August evening. They had closed the inn, as there was no point in keeping it open when the whole village was on its way to the soirée. The road was full of people and carriages. Meyer the auctioneer was at the reins of his two-wheeled gig, a relic of the days of Kaiser Wilhelm the First, with his bulldog at his side. As the horse was as old as the dog, they had to stop on the hills now and again. In one of these pauses, they were overtaken by the butcher in his newly purchased automobile, a 1911 green Daimler, in the back of which the post-lady sat waving cheerfully to everyone. There was an air of expectation about – but also of anxiety. No one was quite sure whether they could trust the rumour about Talbot's return to health and, after all, the moon would be full that night.

But the August sun was still shining now, low over the hills in the west, giving the valley between the village and the mountains a golden glow, and the shadows of the guests were at least five metres long on the road. Crickets chirped along the verges and it was a wonderful evening. But in the hearts of the villagers there was also a tiny cricket of fear sawing away on his violin . . . they had seen too much over the years to walk up to Frankenstein Castle altogether too light-heartedly.

A triumphal archway had been erected in front of the

entrance, woven out of willows and late summer flowers, and on a large banner hanging in the middle was the word WELCOME. The drive in front of the castle was crowded, and several vehicles were already parked there. Among the black and brown carriages glinted the butcher's green Daimler. Horses whinnied, people chatted and there was excitement as well as anxiety in the air.

'Gracious me!' said Irmgard. 'What a lot of people!'

'I think everyone's turned up,' said the innkeeper, his face scarlet and beads of perspiration on his moustache. He was wearing his black suit and bowler in honour of the day, and his stiff collar was torture to him. He turned to his daughter.

'Gretchen, my love,' he said. 'I'm not sure it was really such a good idea for you to come with us. You must promise me to hold Mother's hand all the time ... *should* anything happen.'

'Oh, Otto, don't say that!' said his wife, a delight to the eye in her white lace blouse, red velvet waistcoat and long blue skirt. Her plaits were tied with black silk bows.

In the golden depths of his beer-sodden mind, the guard wished he had a mother whose hand he could hold, but aloud he said to the innkeeper: 'Now, come on, Otto. You mustn't worry the way Helmut does.'

'Who are you to talk about worrying?' said the station-master. He had fortified himself with a whole bottle of Oloroso Fino de Alhambra during the afternoon and his sloping shoulders were unusually straight and determined. He and the guard were also dressed up in black suits and bowler hats.

Hanna Frankenstein was receiving her guests in the hall inside the front door. She was wearing a black costume, a pearl necklace and, in honour of the day, she had had her grey hair blue-tinted a trifle. But she thought it was slightly too blue and that she looked like a very large magpie.

Not one of the guests could compete with her height, except the blacksmith. They all stood there craning their necks as they shook hands with her.

The little guard was there, too, in his bowler hat, which he took off to reveal the usual red mark on his forehead.

'Here we are!' said Hanna Frankenstein. 'Here we have the innkeeper and his family, and the guard and the station-master. Welcome, welcome, gentlemen!' She shook hands with them all and the guard noticed that her hands were in perfect proportion to her feet.

'There are some seats left along the long wall of the banqueting hall,' said Aunt Frankenstein. 'Please take a seat. Igor will show you the way.'

Igor appeared in his ill-fitting old tailcoat, peering up from underneath his fringe of hair, now smoothed down with water and parted in the middle, as he smiled at the guests with his blinding white teeth. The bill from the dentist in Ingolstadt had removed almost all the noughts from Aunt Frankenstein's bank account.

'This way, ladies and gentlemen,' said Igor. 'This way.' He hobbled ahead of them and piloted them into the banqueting hall.

The hall was as large as a football pitch and there were already a few hundred guests seated round the walls. The great stone floor smelt of soap and was strewn with chopped-up juniper, which also threw off its scent. The last rays of the evening sun were falling through the great small-paned windows and Igor was already going round lighting the candles that were placed here and there in man-high candelabra, which he had to stand on tiptoe to reach. Multi-coloured paper garlands were draped across the windows and the walls, and there were also garlands slung across the ceiling. On the far wall was a huge chart of the moon illuminated by a candelabrum on either side. The map's great grey moon gave rise to butterflies in the stomachs of a number of people in the audience. Despite everything, the moon would be full tonight, and a certain Larry Talbot was waiting in the wings.

The post-lady had taken a seat close to the map of the moon and she was scattering calming remarks all round her in a theatrical whisper. The post-lady was in late middle-age, a tall thin lady with a bun at the back of her neck and a slightly turned-up nose. She was looking very nice and was dressed for the evening in a long blood-red dress. Beside her, the butcher sat sweating in his black suit and fiddling nervously at his watch-chain with his large sausage-shaped fingers. The butcher was a widower and for some time there had been chat about him and the post-lady, their ride in the Daimler naturally having started gossip and whisperings among the guests.

The sun had gone down and the hall was almost full. The many candles shone even brighter in the dusk and the tension rose.

Then Meyer the auctioneer appeared with his old bull-dog behind him, and the two of them were shown a seat by the door by Igor. It looked as if all the guests had arrived now and, with her head high, Hanna Frankenstein walked out on to the great floor with a gong in her hand, the juniper crunching under her large boots.

But not all the guests had yet arrived. In the August dusk outside the castle, a black covered carriage came driving up the hill, drawn by two horses lathered with sweat.

Ashen Light

Hanna Frankenstein struck the gong, a fanfare of vibrating brass ringing through the hall, and the crowd fell silent.

'Ladies and Gentlemen,' said Hanna Frankenstein in a loud firm voice. 'I bid you welcome to this little soirée. It gives me great pleasure that so many of you have responded to my invitation ... because we all know that for quite a time the village, both in the present and the past, has been troubled by certain ... irregularities. But Ladies and Gentlemen, all that is now at an end. From now on, things will be different. From now on, Frankenstein Castle will be a centre of science and culture, open to Muses, but not to Horrors.'

The audience applauded.

She went on:

'Tonight I hope the Muses of astronomy and tragedy will hold a protective hand over our little party. And we start the programme with a lecture on the moon by a genuine specialist in the field, Mr Lawrence Talbot.'

She stepped aside and gestured towards the end wall, where Larry Talbot and Frans had entered through a side door, both in dinner jackets. The audience applauded again.

When Aunt Frankenstein retreated through the sea of clapping, she saw another guest arriving, slipping in through the doors, apparently rushed and conscious of his late arrival. He was a dark bearded man of indefinite age, wearing a brown tweed suit and a floppy artist's hat. He looked across the hall to find an empty seat, and Igor hurried up to meet him. When the man took his hat off, he revealed his dark swept-back hair and the deep lines in his forehead. Hanna Frankenstein thought there was something familiar about his face. Where on earth had she seen the man before? The man was given a seat by the door and sat down. Everyone's attention was now riveted on the other end of the hall where Talbot had stepped over to the moon-chart with a pointer in his hand. There was deathly silence in the hall. At any moment, the moon would be rising. More than one member of the audience had checked the time in a diary.

'Mother,' whispered Gretchen. 'Where's the were-wolf?'

The good acoustics of the hall carried her whisper right over to Talbot, who for a moment looked worried. He was already rather pale.

The innkeeper's wife hushed her daughter and whispered back: 'It's that man over by the map. But he doesn't turn into a werewolf any longer.'

'We hope not, anyhow,' whispered the guard, fingering his bowler with sweaty hands.

Larry Talbot licked his dry lips, his eyes flickering over the crowd, the pointer trembling in his hand.

'Ladies and gentlemen,' he said hoarsely. 'If you look out of the window here ...'

He pointed with the pointer and the audience along the east wall turned right round in their seats.

'Then you will see that the full moon is just rising above the mountains.'

They all saw it; like a red balloon, the August moon came sliding up behind the mountains in the east. The sweat began to break out on the palms of more than one pair of hands, stomachs contracted and hearts fluttered ... not least in Hanna Frankenstein. She thought the beating of her heart was thundering out over the hall, as in those famous ghost stories by Edgar Allan Poe. Igor appeared beside her and she leant down and hissed into his ear: 'Keep your fingers crossed, for Heaven's sake.'

'I am, as hard as I can,' he hissed back with a smile. He had taken to smiling all the time now, ever since he had had his new teeth. It was almost unnerving.

'The moon ...' Talbot went on in a hoarse voice. 'The moon is an old acquaintance of us all. It is the earth's nearest grrrrr ... uhum ...'

His voice broke into a growl and he cleared his throat in embarrassment. Aunt Frankenstein could not bear to look any more. She whispered into Igor's ear again: 'Who's that man who's just come in?'

'No idea,' Igor smiled back. 'But he knew my name!'

Talbot struggled on with his moon-chart, the sweat pouring off his face. He took off like a man who stammers, pointing desperately at the full moon with his pointer, like a fencer with a rapier.

'The moon ... is the earth's nearest neighbourrrrrrrrrr ... in space. A cold and inhospitable planet ...'

Gretchen's impatient voice could now be heard all through the hall.

'Mother, won't he *ever* turn into a werewolf?'

'Heaven preserve us,' thought Hanna Frankenstein. 'Why didn't I ban children from the party? Why did I have this party at all?' She began to wonder quite seriously whether she ought to evacuate the whole hall quickly before it was all too late. But she felt sorry for Talbot. This was the chance of a lifetime for him. This was his chance for redress and readjustment to a human life.

'Bravo, Larry!' cried the post-lady encouragingly, and the butcher looked sulky.

The great red balloon of a moon was now right above the mountains, large and challengingly circular as it sailed on outside the window. Talbot's face twitched in a disturbing way and Igor hissed:

'Look, his face is quite ashen.'

As Igor was slightly deaf, his hissed words were louder than he had intended and could be heard all over the hall. An uneasy murmur began to spread along the benches, but Talbot found another thread and desperately started winding it in:

'As I said, the moon is now full ... but at the new moon one can also observe a phenomenon called the ashen light ... ash-grrrrr! Ash-grrrrr ...'

He was off again and an ashen light seemed to lie all over the hall.

'Talbot!' shouted Frans. 'Don't forget the Sea of Tranquillity! The Sea of *Tranquillity*, Talbot!'

'No, exactly,' said Talbot. '*Thank* you. And then there is something called the Sea of Tranquillity ...'

A great calm spread over his pale face. The crisis was over.

But now Aunt Frankenstein's nerves could stand it no longer. She walked across the floor and started clapping.

'An excellent lecture, Mr Talbot,' she said. 'An excellent lecture, short and concise. Thank you very much. Now we know a great deal about the moon that we did not know before. Let us give Mr Talbot a hearty clap.'

Everyone applauded and cheering broke out, the post-lady standing up and crying: 'Bravo, Larry! Bravo!' The butcher looked terribly cross, clapping his sausage fingers with the absolute minimum of sound.

Hanna Frankenstein continued across the floor, calling for silence.

'And now, Ladies and Gentlemen, the second number of the evening.'

Eternally grateful and happy, Talbot staggered out through the side-door and was patted by his second, Frans. A boxer who had just won the heavyweight world championship could not have been sweatier or happier.

Frankenstein Junior and Others

'The second number this evening,' said Hanna Frankenstein. 'As most of you know, the Frankenstein family have certain connections with the great English poet, Shelley or, to be more accurate, with his wife, Mary. This evening, the youngest member of our family, whom I now call Junior, for the first time in history will read a piece of poetry by the aforementioned Shelley. Ladies and Gentlemen ...'

She took a step back and turned to the end wall, thinking in the middle of it all that it was a pity she was only the Master of Ceremonies, when she really wanted to play the main part.

'From Shelley's lyrical poem about the tormented titan, Prometheus, who bursts his bonds, you will now hear an extract of a new interpretation by my excellent secretary, Frans. The person reading this extract is himself a tormented giant, a man who has suffered as Prometheus did, but who has risen again from Purgatory, far fresher than any fabled Phoenix bird.'

'Why did I say that?' she thought. 'What did it sound like? A bit muddled, I imagine, mixing up Prometheus and the Phoenix in that way.'

'Ladies and Gentlemen,' she went on aloud, making a sweeping gesture towards the side-door. '*Frankenstein Junior!*'

The side-door was opened by Frans and a draught whistled through the hall, making the candles flicker. Then heavy footsteps could be heard out there in the darkness, dragging slightly, then coming nearer; sweat again broke out on hundreds of palms, stomachs fluttered and hearts thumped.

An enormous pair of yellow hands appeared ... a huge boot ... another ... and there he was, ducking through the doorway, Frankenstein Junior in Tyrolean costume. A great hum went through the hall, and from the man with a beard came a cry: 'It can't be true!'

'Who *is* that man over there?' whispered Aunt Frankenstein.

Monster stopped in the middle of the floor, his enormous boots apparently even larger now he was wearing shorts. His yellow knees looked like the legs of a very old circus elephant, and at least two clowns could have got into the Tyrolean shorts and still had some room left over. His sleeves were too short and emphasised his great size even more. He had refused to be parted from his jacket. The Tyrolean hat sat on his flat head as if it had been flung up on to a cliff ledge. The cathode and anode glinted in the candlelight.

Monster was holding a piece of paper in front of him in his huge hands. Then he cleared his throat with a noise like thunder and started reading in a deep monotonous sepulchral voice:

'Oh, woe! Alas! pain, pain ever, for ever!'

Gretchen simply could not keep quiet any longer.

'But Mother, why's he wearing Tyrolean costume?'

'I suppose so that he doesn't look horrible,' her mother whispered back. 'Be quiet now.'

There were people in the audience who thought he had

never looked so horrible as he did now, but from over by the door rose a suppressed giggle from the man with a beard. Who was he? Aunt Frankenstein felt she would go mad if she didn't find out soon. There was something so familiar about that face, those deep lines on his forehead and that slightly turned-up nose, and yet she didn't recognise him.

Monster went on with his recital, his deep voice making the windows rattle:

> *'No change, no pause, no hope! Yet I endure*
> *I ask the Earth, have not the mountains felt?*
> *I ask you heaven, the all-beholding sun,*
> *has it not seen? The sea in storm or calm*
> *Heavens ever-changing shadow spread below,*
> *Have its deaf waves not heard my agony?*
> *Ah me! alas, pain, pain ever, for ever.'*

Irmgard leant over to her husband.
'It's really gripping,' she said in a thick voice.
'Yes,' said the innkeeper, his eyes shining. 'We probably weren't very nice to him.'
Monster went on:

> *'He whom some dreadful voice invokes is here*
> *Prometheus, the chained Titan. Horrible forms,*
> *what and who are you? Never yet there came*
> *phantoms so foul through monster-teeming Hell.'*

The guard leant over to the station-master:
'Do you think he means us?'
'One might well wonder,' said his railway colleague.

> *'From the all-miscreative brain of Jove;*
> *Whilst I behold such execrable shapes,*
> *Methinks I grow like what I contemplate*
> *And laugh and stare in loathsome sympathy.'*

'Oh, yes,' said the guard. 'I understood that dig, though it was a subtle one.'

The recital was over. Monster bowed stiffly and retreated.

The applause broke out – a tremendous clapping, people standing on the benches and whistling and shouting, jubilant with happiness and relief now that the tension had gone. Frans and Igor helped to carry out refreshments, a large barrel of beer was dragged on a decorated wheelbarrow into the middle of the floor and a whole battery of lemonade was carried in. Through the jubilant applause, the man in the brown suit thrust his way over to Hanna Frankenstein, his eyes shining above his beard.

'Auntie! Auntie! Absolutely fantastic. I really must congratulate you! What an achievement! What a feat! I am overwhelmed!'

He took her hand and shook it hard.

'Thank you, thank you,' said Aunt Frankenstein with some reserve. 'Excuse me ... but who are you?'

'Don't you recognise me, Auntie? Does my beard really change me that much?'

The voice, the turned-up nose, the eyes ...

'*Henry*!' cried Aunt Frankenstein. 'Henry, you wretch! Is it *you*?'

'Yes, it's me,' laughed Henry Frankenstein. 'Me and none other.'

'Mr Henry!' said Igor, looking like a delighted puppy reunited with his master. 'Welcome back!' he went on, smiling with his white teeth.

'Thank you, Igor, thanks very much. You look at least thirty years younger with those charmer's slabs.'

'Thirty?' said Igor. 'I think I look seventy years younger.'

'I'll send you the dentist's bill later,' said Aunt Frankenstein to Henry. 'Well, you good-for-nothing, back again, are you?' She felt she had to subdue her delight, considering the circumstances. 'Well, I suppose I must bid you welcome ... with some hesitation.'

'I understand your hesitation,' said Henry. 'I understand that. But everything's so different now.'

Then Larry Talbot came over, relaxed and happy, a large tankard of beer in his hand and the post-lady at his heels. The butcher had already left, and they could hear his Daimler starting up with a roar outside the castle.

'Hullo, Henry! So your exile's over, is it?'

'Yes, a rumour reached me about these great successes in all directions, and when I heard about this soirée, I decided ... I came here as quickly as I could. But we nearly arrived too late ...'

'*We?*' said Aunt Frankenstein. 'Surely you haven't got married?'

'No, not me,' said Henry. 'But ... oh, Auntie, Auntie, I have such plans.'

Hanna took half a step backwards, her voice icy cold as she said:

'What? *You*'ve got plans?'

Henry was looking like a delighted schoolboy. His aunt saw that despite his beard, he hadn't grown up one single centimetre. It was the same old good-for-nothing Henry standing in front of her, with his same attitude that life was just one endless irresponsible Christmas Day. She had already mentally begun to pack her bags.

'Auntie,' said Henry. 'It's all so fantastic! And Monster is so changed, too. Junior, I mean. Think how surprised she'll be! Auntie, I swear it'll be the wedding of the century.'

'Henry,' said Aunt Frankenstein icily. 'Please calm

down. What is this wedding you're talking about? And who is *she*? Please speak up now . . . incidentally you look much better without a beard.'

'Auntie, dear, I'm sorry . . . I was so excited by all this. Well, do you remember Dr Pretorius, Auntie?'

'Do you mean,' said Aunt Frankenstein. 'That crazy loon who came here and helped you make a bride for the Monster?'

'Yes, that's right. That's him. A really brilliant man! You should see his home-made dwarfs, Auntie. He keeps them in small glass jars. Oh, they're living works of art. But talking about the bride . . . you know what happened, Auntie. The bride and the Monster didn't take to each other, found no favour, so to speak. That wasn't really all that peculiar, considering what she looked like. I don't mean appearances should matter all that much, but we really did fail there, Pretorius and I. She really did look absolutely frightful, to be honest.'

'Oh, yes?' said Aunt Frankenstein, and an icicle could not have been sharper or colder.

But Henry did not allow his enthusiasm to be chilled. He looked as if he might burst with enthusiasm any minute.

'I expect you're wondering what I've been doing all this time, Auntie?'

Then he dropped the bomb, his eyes shining.

'Oh, Auntie! We've done a face-lift job on the bride! She's sitting out there in my carriage with Dr Pretorius. Come on, Auntie. Come and meet her.'

Hanna Frankenstein raised her large nose a trifle, and ejected one single word:

'*Never!*'

Henry looked like a balloon that had been hit by a blast from a shot gun.

'What?' he said, and you could see and hear the air going out of him.

'I said *never*!' Aunt Frankenstein said again, then she turned to her secretary standing in the crowd, a tankard of beer in his hand. 'Frans! Go and pack your pyjamas and telescope at once! We're leaving tonight.'

'But Auntie,' said Henry. 'She's a beauty! A real smasher! Monster will fall for her in a big way this time. And she'll fall for him ... now he's got so grand and cultured. Auntie! But wait ... why are you leaving, Auntie? Auntie! Come back!'

But Aunt Frankenstein was already on her way, striding up to her room to do her packing.

The party went on without her, the beer flowing, the villagers laughing and shrieking.

Prometheus had indeed burst his chains.

Satisfied with his début as a reciter of poetry, Monster stepped out into the night through a back door to get a breath of fresh air. He had taken off the silly clothes Aunt Frankenstein had insisted on dressing him up in, and was once again wearing his dear old black serge trousers that matched his shrunken jacket so well.

He felt the soft August night caressing his flat skull and stopped to look up at the great red moon. Its red colour brought back a memory in his confused brain ... a dim memory of a woman-like creature he had once met, an unhappy memory of an unsuccessful meeting, a great disappointment. The memory brought with it a great longing in his massive chest, the most important part of which had come from an ex-navvy in Himmelsdorff, a man with a very hot temper. It was an indefinite longing for something red, like the moon, like a pair of lips, like a great disappointment...

He raised his great hands to the moon and suddenly felt as unhappy and lonely as only a monster can. He started stumbling aimlessly on, simply walking, his boots shuffling through the dry grass, the crickets silenced in terror in his path.

Suddenly he was standing in the space in front of the castle, now emptied of people, but full of all kinds of carriages and horses. Harness rustled and hoofs stamped impatiently as the horses caught the strange scent.

Slightly apart from the others was a covered black carriage with lighted lanterns. Monster heard someone talking inside the carriage and thought he recognised the voice ... he quickened his pace, taking great strides, almost tripping over in his haste.

Inside the carriage, a coupé from the turn of the century, sat Dr Pretorius, a man of about sixty with curly reddish hair and a pointed nose with a flat bridge. He was just getting rather irritable because Henry had been so long and it was a great strain sitting and talking reassuringly to the creature sitting beside him. Some automobile maniac had almost scared them both out of their wits just now by revving away down the drive.

The creature was a broad-shouldered woman-like figure with a white face, a pouting blood-red mouth and startling red hair in a sort of giant afro-cut far ahead of its time. She moved her head with small nervous jerky bird-like movements and, when she did so, certain stitches and scars in her skin became clearly visible, though – from a surgical point of view – it was all exemplary needlework. Pretorius really thought the Bride had become a beauty in her revised edition. They had given her the job-description and nickname of Elsa II.

Suddenly Dr Pretorius heard a scraping noise outside the carriage. Henry coming at last, he thought. But it was not Henry. It was another old acquaintance. Monster was looking into the carriage.

And Pretorius saw at that moment they had succeeded.

The electric crackling when contact was made could almost be heard ... love at second sight!

He leapt out of the carriage and ran over to the castle to tell Henry the news, and in the front porch he was almost trampled on by a tall elderly lady dressed in black coming out carrying two suitcases.

All's Well...Everything?

'Igor,' said Hanna Frankenstein. 'Try to get the horse to go a bit faster so that we catch the last night train.'

This time the hay in the cart was nice and dry to sit on, and she dared not smoke for fear of fire. It was a wonderful August night, soft and warm, and the round red moon followed them along the road over the hills. Frans was sitting silently in the hay, his glasses glinting on the tip of his nose in the moonlight.

'Well, you know, Frans,' said Aunt Frankenstein. 'It does seem rather mean to leave so suddenly like this ... but I really do think I've done my bit. It'll be very nice indeed to get back home again, I must say. Did you hear, by the way, that I had a card from Count Dracula today? A really nice card with a picture of a bat on it. He said he had taken my advice and gone back to Transylvania to look for work. He was feeling very well, he said, now that he felt at last that he had a place in society. And do you know what he was working as? On night-duty in a blood-donor centre. The right man in the right place, I should say. But he was a handsome man, he certainly was ...'

'You're very quiet,' she said to Frans. 'Are you upset because we've left?'

'No, I just feel so peculiar,' said Frans bleakly. 'Something to do with the moon ...'

'Well, the way you've stared at it for the last few months, I'm not surprised you feel peculiar. That was a good job done, curing Talbot of his phobias, I really do think so. But it surprises me that you with your scientific aptitude could actually seriously believe that that illusionist was a ghost.'

Frans cleared his throat.

'Gifted as I am, naturally I'm a contradictory individual,' he said, his voice suddenly strangely hoarse.

'Another cold coming!' thought Aunt Frankenstein. 'He will *have* to go to a specialist when we get home.'

They drove on for a while in silence, no sound except the tap of hoofs and the creaking of the cart, the moon following them on their journey, its treacherous light falling on to Frans's pale face.

'Frans,' said Aunt Frankenstein. 'Didn't you say you had shaved just before our guests arrived?'

'The Sea of Tranquillity ... the Sea of Serenity ...' mumbled Frans hoarsely.

'Your whole face is hairy!' said Aunt Frankenstein.

Frans was staring at the moon, gabbling away to himself.

'The Sea of Tranquillity ... Mare Tranquillitatis ... Marrrrrre Trrrrrranqu ...'

His voice broke into a growl.

When Hanna Frankenstein looked closer at him, she saw that hair was growing all over the man, on his hands as well, and the nails he usually kept so praiseworthily short were suddenly as long as Struwelpeter's.

'But Frans!' she cried. 'What's the matter? Your lower jaw is just like Talbot's. Aren't you ashamed of yourself? An astronomer and all.'

Frans just growled in reply.

She tugged at Igor's coat-tails.

'Igor!' she cried. 'Stop! I've had enough. I want to get down.'

Igor turned round, his new teeth gleaming white in the moonlight, now protruding like skittles out of his lower lip in his hairy face, and he growled at her in reply.

Then Aunt Frankenstein picked up her suitcases and jumped right out of this story.